THE GHOST FRONT

THE GHOST FRONT

by Frank Bonham

E. P. DUTTON & CO., INC., NEW YORK

Fourth Printing June 1974

Library of Congress Catalog Card Number: 67-20122

Map by Veit-Martin Associates

To Charles I. Coombs,
with appreciation

Contents

8   Contents

THE ARDENNES FRONT, NORTH

Foreword

The Ardennes Front, that dark December of 1944, was a place of cold and silence, a lovely if frigid rest area along the eighty-five-mile foxhole line between Belgium and Germany. Both American and German commanders used it as a region in which to train new units and allow battle-weary ones a chance to recuperate.

Men of newer divisions, like the green 106th Infantry Division, first of the eighteen-year-old draftees, worried about the coming and going of so many German soldiers through the woods. And what about the reports of whole regiments of Nazi storm troopers bivouacked in the villages near the front? Of monstrous King Tiger tanks parked in barns, and trucks creeping on beds of straw along narrow roads with supplies for a major assault?

Intelligence officers at Allied supreme headquarters reassured them. There were always such scare stories. But the facts should encourage them.

Since D day—June 6, 1944—the *Wehrmacht* had been driven from the beaches of Normandy to their own borders. Of the German air force, only a few hundred fighter craft were left. The Nazi ground forces were too exhausted and sick to stage an assault of any kind.

Believe us, said Intelligence, the Germans are content to let us do all the assaulting!

Then, as a foggy dawn broke on 16 December, the long, twisting Ardennes line exploded with what was to be Adolf Hitler's most ambitious assault of the war.

Within a few days, a quarter of a million Nazi soldiers, one thousand tanks and assault guns, and nearly two thousand artillery pieces had driven so deeply into the American line that correspondents, looking at the battle maps, referred to the counteroffensive as the "Battle of the Bulge."

The Ghost Front is a novel based on actual battles and combat actions of this last—and greatest—German offensive of World War II; and of the fate of one division in particular, the ill-starred "Golden Lions" of the 106th.

THE GHOST FRONT

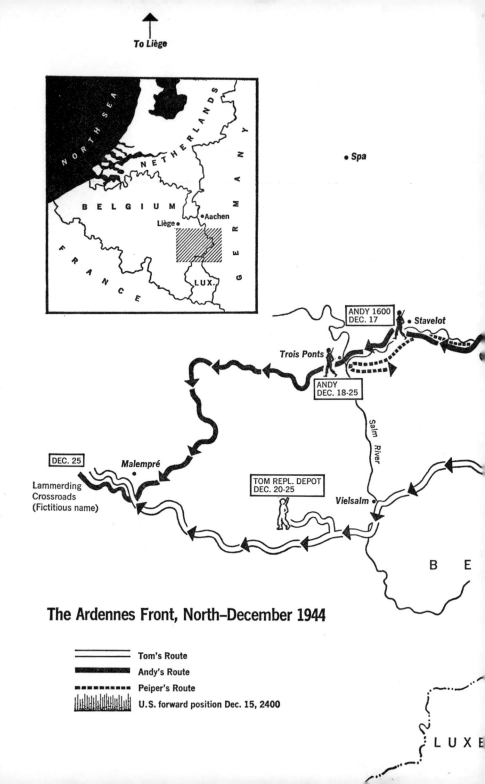

To Liège

NORTH SEA

NETHERLANDS

GERMANY

BELGIUM

FRANCE

Liège • Aachen

LUX.

• Spa

ANDY 1600
DEC. 17

• Stavelot

Trois Ponts

ANDY
DEC. 18-25

Salm River

DEC. 25

Malempré •

Lammerding
Crossroads
(Fictitious name)

TOM REPL. DEPOT
DEC. 20-25

Vielsalm •

B   E

The Ardennes Front, North–December 1944

──────── Tom's Route

━━━━━━━━ Andy's Route

▬ ▬ ▬ ▬ Peiper's Route

⫶⫶⫶⫶⫶⫶⫶⫶ U.S. forward position Dec. 15, 2400

LUXE

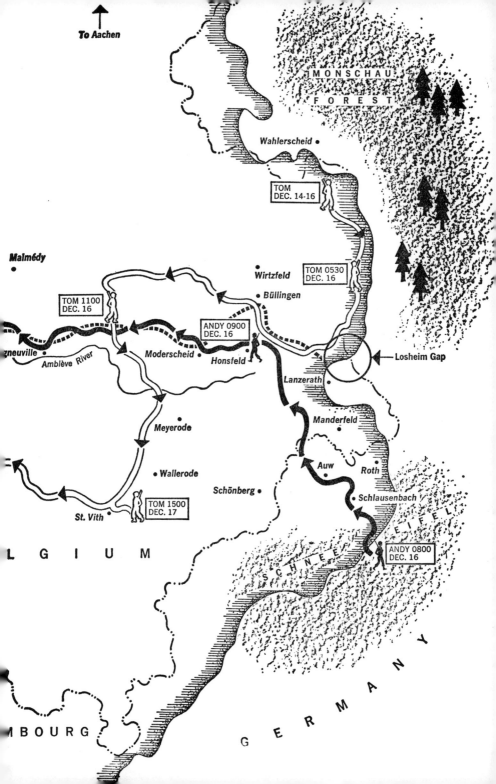

PART ONE

The Snow Mountains

Near the northern end of the Ardennes Front lay the quietest, loveliest sector of the line: the Schnee Eifel, or Snow Mountains. Picture-postcard villages nestled in deep river valleys or perched like eagles' nests on bald ridges.

The exhausted veterans of the 2nd Infantry Division, resting here, felt that they had landed in a refrigerated heaven. But early in December they were suddenly displaced by a division of shivering untried warriors.

Fresh from field exercises in England, the Golden Lions of the 106th Infantry were unappreciative of their good fortune. Rations were cold, and they had no overshoes! Already there were many cases of trench foot. Their winterized huts were damp and smelly. And what about Christmas parcels? Having been so recently transferred, they were certain that their gifts would not arrive before St. Patrick's Day.

Grousing and groaning, they settled down to the cold and monotony, dreaming fondly of the muddy training camp in England that they had just left. . . .

CHAPTER ONE

Training Camp
Banbury, England
8 December

All day Andy Croft had crawled around in the English mud under barbed wire, while live ammunition zipped over his head and simulated artillery bursts hurled clods upon him. After Retreat, he had showered, cleaned his muddy GI spectacles that, perched on his bony nose, gave him somewhat the look of an intelligent crow, and hurried off to visit his brother in the camp hospital.

He was waiting now for the desk clerk to finish a telephone conversation and notice him. In fifteen minutes he was due back in the company area to watch a training film on bayonet fighting. In growing anxiety, he shifted from one foot to the other, nibbling the inside of his lower lip and glancing frequently at the clock, which he checked occasionally against his wristwatch. He was a tall, hungry-looking youth with a prominent Adam's apple and a narrow face.

The clerk hung up.

"Request permission to visit my brother," Andy said breathlessly. "He's in—"

"Name?"

"Tom—Thomas Croft. Ward 82A."

"Go ahead."

Andy hurried down a long cream-colored hall, turned left, then right. He knew every turn in the corridor, having visited his brother every night since he had cut his foot in the showers two weeks ago. In all their eighteen years, the Croft twins had never before been separated. The experience was a disturbing one for Andy. If he had not known it before, he realized now that Tom was the decision-making part of their team. He found himself reluctant to take action, whether it involved having seconds in the mess hall or pulling the pin on a practice grenade.

Well, it was natural, he had told himself. Even the Army, understanding about twins, had assigned them to the same training battalion in California when they enlisted after high school graduation. The kindly old recruiting sergeant who took their applications promised faithfully that they would always be kept together. It was almost like getting married.

Much to Andy's surprise, they had been kept together. He had expected the worst of the Army, from the day Tom started talking about enlistment.

"Why don't we go down and get it over with?" Tom argued. "They'll draft us anyway, and if we get in now we'll have first shot at a lot of great souvenirs."

But Andy remembered a souvenir their uncle had brought back from World War I: a lung weakened by mustard gas. Besides, he was engrossed in a backyard scientific project. Would string beans grown on a slowly revolving turntable distort themselves in an effort to face the light?

But though he presented feeble arguments for waiting to be drafted, all the logic was on Tom's side. The Japanese were on the run; the Germans, after the Normandy invasion, in full retreat across France. Behind them they left entire divisions slaughtered and captured. There was no doubt whatever that the war was all but finished.

So, sadly, Andy planted the pale, perplexed bean sprouts in the garden, and went off to war with his brother.

In Ward 82A, men in maroon-colored bathrobes drifted about in boredom. Others lay on their cots, smoking, talking, or reading. Few of the men in the long barracks-like room looked very sick, Tom least of all. He had been trying for a week to get out. He bounded from his cot as Andy entered. Several inches shorter than Andy, he was blond, square-shouldered, strong, a natural athlete. A certain fetching ruggedness was given to his features by a nose broken in football.

"What's the scoop?" he demanded.

"Nothing new, Tommy. How's the foot?"

"Same. The luck of the Crofts," Tom said bitterly. "Crawl a mile through barbed wire and mud, get blown off the ground by a simulated land mine—then step on a broken bay-rum bottle in the shower! Did you get the things I told you to?"

Andy nodded, and sat on the cot. Groping inside his raincoat, he conjured up a tablet of writing paper, an envelope, a ball-point pen, and a block of English postage stamps. Tom flipped up the cover of the tablet. The Great Seal of the Army of the United States, gold-embossed, adorned each page of the stationery. He looked up in disgust.

"Holy cow! Couldn't you find something a little crummier?"

"It's all the PX carries," Andy said humbly.

Tom linked his hands on top of his head and glared down the ward.

"The Great Seal! The idea was for this letter to come through the regular mail—to look as *un*-Army as possible. If

Colonel Purdy knows it's from a patient, he'll throw it out like everything else I've sent through channels."

Andy grinned. "You know what they say: The only thing harder than getting into an Army hospital is getting out."

"Says who?"

"Shanks. Hey, he made Private first class yesterday!"

"Well, fabulous," Tom said bitterly. "I'm so happy for him. The Mouth makes Pfc., while I play checkers with idiots."

"If there's still infection," Andy said, "maybe you shouldn't be out anyway."

"It'll heal outside as well as inside."

Down the line, a radio was playing *"Tangerine, she's the sweetest one—"* Another blared *"To the everlasting glory of the infantry!"* A lanky, bathrobed ruin of fifty years or more leaned against the foot of Tom's bed, surreptitiously rattling some dice in his pocket.

"Acey-deucey-dicey!" he chanted. "Come on, kid—we know you're loaded. Shoot a buck!"

Tom waved him off. The man drifted away like a beggar, chanting the same prayer at the next bed.

"Oh, I tell you, brother!" Tom said. "You can't appreciate a well-run madhouse till you spend three weeks in *this* ward."

"Rotunno knows a guy that's been in Ward 14 for a month with athlete's foot."

"While guys with temperatures of 110 are scratching at the windows trying to get in!"

Andy looked at his wristwatch. "Listen, Tommy, I've got to take off. We've got a training film tonight."

"On what?"

"Bayonet."

Tom made comical jabbing motions with both hands clenched together. "Long *thrust!* Short *thrust!* Are they still teaching *bayonet,* for Pete's sake, with the war practically over?"

Andy grinned. Confinement had soured Tom so that he did not even sound like himself. He had loved the training from the start, even the long hikes. He was proud of their brand-new division, the 106th Infantry. It was the highest numbered unit in the Army, with the lowest average age, for the Golden Lion Division was loaded with the first of the eighteen-year-old draftees.

Tom rose as Andy picked up his helmet. "How about the CO? Did you talk to him?"

"I'll do it tomorrow. We've been in the field every day, and after dinner he's always left. I talked to Sergeant Brocius, though—"

"*That* bucket of blubber! Listen, Tiger," Tom exhorted, clutching his arm, "get on the ball! See somebody! If you leave without me, you'll have about as much chance as a ventriloquist's dummy with the ventriloquist on vacation."

Andy's face reddened. "Okay, bright boy! Why don't you think your own way out of here?"

Immediately Tom smiled and punched his shoulder. "Atta-boy, kid! That's what I wanted to hear. Now take that spirit back and build a fire under somebody."

Through the dripping English mist, Andy trotted back to the company area. He was resentful of the ventriloquist joke, knowing that it was true.

Perhaps because Tom had been born a half hour earlier, he had seized an advantage he had never relinquished. His spoon was always first in the Pablum, his bicycle out ahead, his voice louder in any game. People liked him immediately. They learned to like Andy over a period of time. It had not mattered much until they went into the Army. Then Andy had begun to realize that, in many ways, he was helpless without his brother. He could not imagine making important decisions without consulting the other half of his will, encased in Tom's skull.

He stopped at the mess hall, but the door was locked; he was too late even for a handout. He trudged along the wet duckboards to the crowded post exchange and bought some cheese nips and candy bars. A soldier in the crowd called to him as he was leaving.

"*Oye, amigo!*"

Andy turned to look into the flat Eskimo-like features of Joseph Celaya, an Indian boy from Arizona. Everybody called him Apache. Apache was carrying candy bars, too.

"You didn't miss anything tonight," he said. "I've eaten better chow in cow camps. How's Tom?"

"About the same. Still going crazy trying to get out."

Apache unwrapped a candy bar. "For two fox skins, I'll do the Elk Dance for you. According to my uncle, it'll make cars start, sprout corn, and open jailhouse doors."

"I'll give you four skins," Andy said gloomily. "Do it twice."

Apache looked at him in curiosity. "Maybe I'm stupid, kid. But if he doesn't get out this week, he'll get out next. So what's the rush?"

"What if we ship out this week?" Andy said.

"Then he'll catch up with us later."

Andy hesitated; he was embarrassed to speak of what was so close to him. "Well, I—I kind of expect him to make up my mind for me, I guess."

"About what?" Apache seemed puzzled. Suddenly Andy decided to blurt it out and think later.

"About everything! At home, I couldn't even dress in the morning until I saw what he was going to wear. After class

I'd always look for him in the hall—just touching base, making sure he was still around."

To his relief, Apache did not laugh. He appeared more puzzled than amused.

"I've heard about twins," he said, "but what you're talking about sounds like Siamese twins."

"That's it," Andy said bitterly. "We're attached at the brain. At least I'm attached to him."

Apache laughed. "Forget it, kid. It's all in the head. You've done as good as Tom has in the training. Plus," he pointed out, "you've got a language specialty. So you've actually done better than he has. Right?"

Andy blew a raindrop from his nose. "No, I just happened to take to languages, like he takes to sports. We had a German baby-sitter when we were little. So I knew German about as soon as I knew English."

"What about him? Didn't he have the same baby-sitter?"

"He learned too, but he's forgotten most of it."

There was silence. Apache contentedly munched the candy bar as they walked. Andy suppressed a sigh. It was clear that he might as well not have mentioned his problem. For, after all, how could anyone else comprehend something you couldn't explain even to yourself?

The rain began to fall more heavily. They trotted the last fifty feet to the barracks. Gleaming like trout, they hurried inside. There they halted in surprise.

The long, dim barracks resounded to the clamor of thirty men hastily rolling packs and stowing gear in barracks bags. Terry Shanks—the Mouth—made the quickstep sign at them.

"On the double!" he bawled. "We ship in the morning."

A flash of heat and cold left Andy dizzy. Suddenly he turned and left the barracks.

He ran all the way back to the orderly room. At his desk, First Sergeant Brocius was typing a list of names and smoking a cigar. "Request permission to see the commanding officer!" Andy panted.

Brocius rubbed off his cigar ash in a can lid. "Negative on that," he said in his burlap voice.

Andy wiped his nose on his wet mitten. "Listen, Sergeant—"

"No, *you* listen, Private. We ship out in the morning. You haven't got time to chat with Captain Potter, and he don't have time for you."

"Sergeant, my brother and I are supposed to stay together. It—It's an Army regulation." He thrust out his chin. "Do I stay here, or does he go along?"

"That's the choice you give me, huh?" Sergeant Brocius puffed thoughtfully on his cigar. "Okay, Croft. I'll staple your 201 files together, just like Mutt and Jeff. If he don't make the ship, he'll follow as soon as he gets his health back."

Before dawn, the division boarded ships and left England. Hours later, the seasick troops shuffled down the gangplanks, humpbacked with gear, their young faces pinched with cold and misery, to form up in a muddy field on the coast of France.

Andy whispered to Apache: "Do the Elk Dance! I'll pay double."

Apache glumly jigged around in the mud.

Soon, on empty stomachs, they were prodded into open trucks like cattle. Off they rolled, through the dripping French countryside, in the general direction of combat. Apache leaned toward Andy and tapped his shoulder.

"Cheer up," he said. "Remember—you speak the language. If you can't kill Germans, you can plead with them."

CHAPTER TWO

The Schnee Eifel
Near Schlausenbach, Germany
11 December

For two days the division traveled in frozen misery across France and Belgium. Near dark on the second day they rolled through a belt of barbed wire and concrete pyramids, a section of Germany's famous Siegfried Line—the *Westwall* at its borders, which, the Nazis had boasted, no enemy would ever penetrate. But GI's had smashed it here with tanks, artillery, and bayonets. Awed and uneasy, Andy looked at the burned-out tanks, demolished fieldpieces, and incinerated bunkers among the trees.

In a tiny mountain village that night, MP's began directing the three regiments of the 106th Division north and south into the line. There was a sense of rush and confusion. Officers strode up and down, shouting.

"*First* Platoon! Who the devil sent them out on *that* road!"

"Where's Sergeant Brand? I specifically told him to *wait here!*"

But, little by little, the huge lump of battle iron called the 106th Infantry was broken up and scattered throughout the mountains according to some mysterious design. Behind the truck carrying most of Andy's platoon glimmered the blue cat's-eye headlamps of the jeep carrying their platoon leader, Lieutenant Sizemore. Andy could see no other vehicles. The truck halted in a dark wood.

A roar of wind in huge firs came up. Andy tried to see where they were, but the woods were too dense and it was foggy. The jeep rolled up; a burly noncom trotted from the trees to salute Lieutenant Sizemore, sitting beside his driver.

"Sergeant Nava, Lieutenant. Are you 3rd Platoon, Fox Company?"

"We're two squads of 3rd, Sergeant, plus a weapons squad."

"That's all?"

"So far. We'll be spread out pretty thin for a while."

The sergeant was big and bearish and spoke with a faint accent. "I'd suggest leaving the truck here, sir, so the Jerries won't hear the engine and know we're switching. I'll show you up to the command post and the squad huts."

Andy's knees began to quake. Jerries! Within earshot? What went on?

"Is there hot coffee for the men?" asked the lieutenant.

"No, sir. They took the mess truck away this morning. We're on cold rations."

"What about the troops we're relieving?"

"Ready to travel. I was the platoon sergeant here. I'm attached to your platoon, now. Don't ask me why, sir," Nava added glumly.

Lieutenant Sizemore counted heads. He had joined the outfit shortly before it shipped out, a capable young officer who was rumored (like most officers) to have attended West Point. At the lieutenant's command, Sergeant Nava formed the men into a column of twos and marched them to a log bunker sunk in the earth.

"This is your command post, Lieutenant," he said. "There's

only one telephone operating. To report to Battalion, you'll have to call Regiment, at Schlausenbach, and get them to forward the message to Battalion. Schlausenbach's about four miles west of us."

"Oh, my aching—! What about lines to our outposts and the strongpoints on our flanks?"

"Wire's laid from here to Washington, sir, but 2nd Division took all its telephones along. I managed to hide one out for you. We'll have to use radio to the outposts."

As the lieutenant ducked into the shelter, Sergeant Nava led the troops into a wind pouring down a bare slope. Glazed with old snow, the ground swept up to a bald ridge. Just under the ridge a Sherman tank was dug in for use as an artillery piece. A group of gaunt, subhuman veterans standing beside it jeered at the teen-age soldiers as they passed. Andy brushed by one with a famished-looking face, black whisker stubble, sunken eyes, and a sardonic mouth. He looked deathly tired, actually sick, as he croaked:

"Give 'em hell, Boy Scouts!"

"Sic 'em, Lions!" another man called.

"Mee-yow!"

"What'd they feed them Lions on—milk toast?" another voice asked. "I don't think they got their permanent teeth yet."

Shanks jeered back: "You know what a 2nd Division dog-face is?—a One-oh-six man with his brains knocked out!"

The veterans shouted obscenities.

The sergeant marched the detachment along the ridge, dropping two or three men at each half-buried hut. Andy and Apache were quartered midway along the ridge. The remaining men trudged into the windy darkness. A chill shook Andy. He groped down the steps of the shelter and moved a blackout blanket aside. Dampness and mildew puffed out at him. He found matches and struck a light.

The dirt floor was littered with old ration boxes and trash. Crude bunks were slung from the walls. There was a smell of mice and sweaty underwear. Tin cans full of cigarette butts rested on every surface. He thought of his room at home: Model planes hanging on threads tacked to the ceiling, books on a shelf, a comfortable disorder of clothing, sports equipment, souvenirs of games and outings.

"Hey—a stove!" Apache said. Andy looked. A miniature woodstove squatted in one corner, a few scraps of wood beside it. Apache dropped his pack. "Let's crawl in. Just as liable as not to draw guard duty tonight."

Andy picked a bunk near the door, then changed his mind and carried his gear to another. For a moment he had forgotten that Tom always liked to be near the door. Tom would be along any day, he was sure, and there was no use having to move.

Apache was trying to build a fire in the tiny woodstove when Andy awoke. Cracks of light pierced the blackout blanket and gleamed in the rifle slots high in the wall. Andy gazed around, puffy-eyed and dull, unable to grasp where he was. Then he sat up with a grunt, shocked by the recollection that he was within a few hundred yards of the German line.

Apache looked back over his shoulder, an irregular lump of olive-drab clothing topped by a round brown face under a knitted woolen cap.

"Chihuahua, it's cold!" He shivered. "Those doughs didn't leave enough firewood to fry an egg. And what they left won't burn."

A sweetish white smoke leaked out of the stove. He fanned

the draft with his hand. "Have you looked outside?" Andy asked, lifting his spectacles from a nail where he had hung them.

"Yeah. It's pretty country, but the weather's lousy."

"Seen any of the other guys?"

"No. Everybody's out of sight."

Andy fumbled with his laces. The frigid air thickened his mind as well as his blood. Rising, he milled his arms to get his blood circulating. "Tom will probably like it here. He likes to ski. I suppose he'll be along about tonight—tomorrow, maybe. . . ."

Apache gave him a glance, then said quickly: "Look through the rifle loops. You can see most of this ridge we're on."

Andy stood on a ledge to peer through a slot between two logs. Cold wind hissed against his eyes. They were on a stony ridge where a few stunted trees clung. The vague shapes of rifle and machine-gun emplacements were visible among ragged scraps of snow. Eastward, the ridge slid like a ski slope down into a wide valley. Hillside farms patterned the slope. Beneath a sodden covering of clouds, he saw a village caught in the elbow of a river, the spire of a church pressing up through trees.

There was a sound of running feet and a jingle of equipment. They turned, startled, as a burly soldier whipped the blackout curtain aside. It was Sergeant Nava, his dark features wrathful.

"What are you idiots doing—sending up smoke signals?"

Apache gestured weakly. "How come the stove, Sergeant, if we can't use it?"

"It's for night, idiot, when the enemy can't see the smoke! Pull out that fuel and stamp it into the floor."

While they trampled the smoking branches, he stood at a

rifle slot, scrutinizing the valley below. "Abe," he said, apparently to himself, "we'll be lucky if we don't catch some 88's."

But no shells came, and he finally turned. He had features like rock, chiseled and earth-brown. His jaw was solid, his neck thick, his head tilted forward as if to butt. There was a quirk to his eyebrows that made him look perpetually surprised.

"How long have you bolos been in the Army?" he asked.

"Six months," Andy mumbled.

"Is the whole outfit as young as you?"

"Most of us," Apache said. "Shanks is older. He's twenty."

Nava nodded solemnly. "It's good to have a few gray hairs in the outfit. Makes for steadiness in the younger men. Fall out in five minutes by the tank."

As the blanket fell in place behind him, they heard him talking to himself. "Abe, you poor slob! With thirteen million people in uniform, you wind up with a high school chess team!"

They pulled on overcoats, grabbed rifles, and hurried down the hill. From what Andy could see, the defenses consisted primarily of weapon emplacements and some slit trenches on the ridge, protected by concertinas of barbed wire. Heavy mortars and antitank guns were hidden on the backslope.

The men straggled down to the Sherman tank, two squads of riflemen and a heavy-weapons squad, less a few men on watch. Moving about to keep warm, they joked nervously about their quarters and probable duties, until Sergeant Nava came in view, hiking up the hill from the trees. Nava climbed with a hulking bull-like gait. He brought them to attention and formed them into ranks. Finally he called the roll from a slip of paper, looking intently at each man as he answered.

". . . Pettis, William Junior."

"Here!"

It was the piping voice of Junior Pettis, who could have passed for a Boy Scout in any army. Nava stared at him, his brows quirking.

"How'd you get in the Army, Pettis?"

Junior, who blushed easily, reddened from scarf to helmet. "I lied about my age. I said I was sixty, but they took me anyway."

Nava scratched his chin. "I think the U.S. Army may have grounds for a suit against your parents, Pettis. If you're over sixteen, I'm Pancho Villa."

He looked at the slip of paper again. "Newcomb, Paul?" He was beginning to sound apprehensive.

Andy frowned. Newcomb? Never heard of him. He must have been jammed into the truck at some checkpoint last night.

An old man's voice answered. "Here, Sergeant, sir."

Nava looked in shock at the old man in the front rank; his hands fell to his sides. Andy craned his neck to see the man —and grinned. Everyone was chuckling. Newcomb was at least sixty, a red-faced old-timer with a large, naked-looking nose and the features of an amiable buzzard. His eyes were dim moonstones hung in loops of pink skin.

"Somebody must be kidding!" Nava said in disbelief. "Old men and kids! Pop, what the hell are *you* doing up here?"

"Beats me, Sergeant. I joined up for Army Post Office. Served in APO in the last war. I'm a professional mailman. They said I'd be in 106th Division headquarters. I was attached to 422nd Regiment for rations and quarters till they wanted me."

"Had basic?"

"Yup. Come through like a kid." Pop winked at the others.

Lieutenant Sizemore came in view, hiking down from the ridge. Nava muttered something to himself and brought the detachment to attention again. Sizemore took his place and looked the group over.

"At ease, men. In case you haven't heard, this is Strongpoint Dragonfly. We've got two miles to patrol. These mountains are called the Schnee Eifel. That means Snow Mountains. It looks like a nice place to spend Christmas, and in fact, we'll probably still be here next spring. Any questions?"

Everyone was too cold and befuddled to formulate the great question: *Will we have to fight?*

Andy raised his hand. "What's a strongpoint, sir?"

The other men chuckled. But the lieutenant did not crack a smile.

"That's a good question. A strongpoint takes the place of a line, when you're spread out thin. We have machine guns, mortars, two tanks, and some antitank guns, and our front is protected by barbed wire and mines. Two miles north is Strongpoint Warcry. Two miles south is Nighthawk. We'll run contact patrols every two hours."

Pfc. Terry Shanks raised his arm. The Mouth was big and blond, as sturdy as a Scandinavian woodcutter, and with a long, horselike face. Lieutenant Sizemore recognized him.

"Sir, is this what they call a positional defense?"

Andy knew it must be, or the Mouth would not have asked.

"That is correct," said the lieutenant. "Mobility is the key to a defense like this. We can move anywhere we're needed at a moment's notice. You'll be glad to know that they call this 'the Ghost Front.' The Germans are spread out as thin as we are. Neither side wants to fight. Both of us use the area to train new units and test them in, er, combat situations."

Blooding, they called it, Andy remembered. He gulped.

"Sergeant Nava," said the officer, "will you fill the men in on the general situation?"

The sergeant straightened, bringing the barrel of his slung tommy gun up vertically like an antenna.

"Yes, sir. I don't buy that 'Ghost Front,' because the ghost walks around here every day. You'll see Kraut patrols as often as you see the mailman at home. Germans have even been seen visiting in villages behind us. When there's a contact, the policy is to observe a gentleman's agreement, and not fire. But one of these days we'll run into some Jerries who aren't gentlemen, and there'll be firing. So we go ready. Every patrol we make will be a combat patrol."

"Can you tell the men something about their opposite numbers in the German lines?" Lieutenant Sizemore suggested.

Nava's brow corrugated. There was something Stone Age about the bar-like prominence of it.

"Some are kids, some are old men, some are veterans from the Russian Front who catch bullets in their teeth and spit them back at you. Most of them have lice and trench foot, and their teeth are falling out. But there's one thing they all have: clean rifles. When we capture one, his weapon is clean and fully loaded. That's a pretty good measure of a soldier."

He closed his mouth in such a way that they knew his speech was over.

The lieutenant again took over, glancing at a sheaf of paper. "Croft, Andrew—raise your hand. Your file says you speak German. Do you have conversational ability?"

"Yes, sir. My brother and I had a lady who—well—a baby-sitter—and she spoke German to us."

The squad was laughing. Andy looked around and grinned sheepishly. Nava shook his head pessimistically, and the lieutenant smiled.

"Very good. Show me a soldier who had a German baby-sitter, and I'll show you one who goes along on all the patrols. Sergeant, I want two-hour contact patrols run. At 0900, one patrol will go north, one south. Patrols from adjacent strongpoints will meet you."

Because of the extreme shortage of men, the sergeant had to break up the two twelve-man rifle squads into three. The heavy-weapons squad, as specialists, were excused from patrol duty. While contact patrols were run, the extra squad would man the outposts behind the barbed wire. Andy tried not to shiver while Nava morosely inspected the squad he was taking out on patrol. Eight anxious young faces peered from bundles of winter clothing and overlarge helmets. Nava shook his head, waved his arm, and trudged north. The patrol hustled close behind him until he threw back an irritated glance.

"Don't bunch up, idiots."

The trail switched in and out of thickets and stands of twisted trees. Below the ridge lay hillside farms crisscrossed with stone fences and marbled with snow. The cleared land was bounded by dense stands of timber. The cold breeze brought the bark of an engine. Tilting his helmet, the sergeant listened.

"Tanks!" he muttered.

"Maybe it's just trucks, Sergeant," said Shanks.

"Tanks," Nava repeated. Then: "How come, Abe? What are those lousy Krauts up to now?"

Andy was fascinated by his soliloquies. Nava seemed to have a strong and intimate relationship with someone called Abe, who of course was himself. If you were around him enough, he supposed, you would soon know every thought in his head.

Vito Rotunno whispered to Andy. He was short and fat, with a nose like a small olive-tinged banana. "He's nuts! Always talking to himself."

Shanks walked up to Sergeant Nava, insinuating himself into the command picture. "Wouldn't they be expected to have some tanks, Sarge?" he asked.

"The Jerries don't have enough armor to waste in an area like this. Intelligence says they've only got two horse-drawn fieldpieces opposite us. Some night we're going down there and report them for overworking those horses."

The patrol trailed into a frosty blind of undergrowth. Everyone was as nervous as a cat. Andy bumped into Junior, who had stopped short. "For Pete's sake—" Then he saw the sergeant signaling: *Take cover!* He relayed the signal and flopped under a bush, his rifle at his shoulder.

For a half-minute there was silence. Andy's heart pounded so hard he felt as though he would choke to death.

"On your feet," the sergeant called, at last. "It's the patrol from Warcry."

As the two groups met, Sergeant Nava gave a shout. He had recognized the sergeant commanding the other squad.

"Hey, Murph! You running a boys' club, too?"

The other man, bulky and awkward in his short coat and heavy pants, grinned. "I volunteered for hazardous duty, Abe. That is what I drew. You got any telephones?"

"Only the one I hid out."

"Situation normal," Murphy said. They walked off together to study the valley and hold a private conversation. As they returned, Andy heard Nava saying:

"Plus, I hear engines all the time. S-2 says the Jerries are playing records of tanks to keep us guessing. Maybe so. But I wish we'd play some howitzer music back at them."

"You take things too serious, Abe," said Murphy. "Any way you look at it, this Ghost Front deal beats fighting."

Nava stabbed a stiff forefinger at him. "You get yourself a map and study it sometime. Look at that pass north of here. If the Krauts made a big attack, that's where they'd come. Push through, turn north and south, and cut us off. Right?"

"Right. But they're not coming—they're still going. Who's feeding you all this big-attack garbage?"

"The new CO—Lieutenant Sizemore," Nava said frankly. "He says every time the Germans have started a war, they've come through that pass—the Losheim Gap. Franco-Prussian War, World War I, this one."

"Has this lieutenant ever been in combat?"

"No. But he's got plenty up here."

Murphy clapped him on the shoulder. "You've got something up there too, Abe—dandruff. Bring your maps along tomorrow. We'll plan us a trip."

PART TWO

The Terrible Forest

North of the Schnee Eifel was a place of death and horror called the Monschau Forest. For weeks American infantry struggling to capture the Roer dams had taken such losses here that a war correspondent named Ernest Hemingway said pessimistically:

"It would save everybody a lot of trouble if we just machine-gunned replacements as they climbed out of the trucks."

One of the hardest hit of all the bleeding divisions was 2nd Infantry, only recently brought back from a brief convalescence in the Schnee Eifel. Desperate for men, the 2nd's commanders would accept anything that could fight—a squad, a platoon, a company borrowed from another division in reserve. Even discharged hospital patients on the way to rejoin their outfits were in danger of landing, instead, in a 2nd Division unit in the nightmarish Monschau Forest. . . .

CHAPTER THREE

Training Camp
Banbury, England
10 December

Forty-eight hours after the Golden Lions left England, a doctor stopped at the foot of Tom Croft's hospital bed. He compared the name on the bed tag with that on a chart he carried, and shot Tom a glance of suspicion.

"How's the foot, soldier?"

Tom laid aside a book he had been reading, kicked off his slipper, and silently raised his foot. He blamed the entire medical department for the atrocity of benching him when his outfit shipped out, and he had decided to have as little to do with any of the doctors or medics as possible.

The doctor traced the jagged pink line across his heel, and straightened. "There's nothing wrong with your foot," he announced. "It's healed perfectly. I'm going to return you to duty."

Tom's heart gave a huge throb, but he suppressed his joy, realizing that if he betrayed pleasure at being returned to duty he might very well go to the psychiatric ward for observation instead.

"I don't know, sir," he said. "It still hurts sometimes."

Already scribbling on Tom's chart, the doctor snapped, "I wasn't *asking* how you felt, soldier—I was *telling* you."

The bugles of the camp were blowing Retreat as Tom ran up the steps of the barracks, grinning to himself. A few of the boys *must* still be here! They would all go over together. But his shoulders sagged as he opened the door. The dark hall was deserted. Only one cot was made up: his own, with his gear piled on it.

He went to the orderly room to ask for word of the division. Even the old clerks were gone. New cadremen had usurped their desks. A clerk told him to come back in the morning.

"We ought to know where you're going by then."

He passed the night in cold loneliness. The rows of unmade cots depressed him. The ghosts of 3rd Platoon roamed the aisle and yelled in the showers: The Mouth, asking who had left his socks on his bed; Rotunno, eating and complaining; Junior, lost in mental mists. Andy . . .

Poor kid, he thought. Bet he's out of his mind.

In the morning he checked again with the orderly room clerk. To his surprise, his shipping orders were ready.

"Pack and run," the clerk said. "Hitch a ride to the docks and get on a boat. You're joining your unit in Belgium."

Tom smacked his fist against his hand. Then he paused. "Belgium? How'd they get there so fast?"

"They've been there for months. Weren't they in on the invasion?"

Tom peered at him doubtfully. "Are you kidding? We were still in high school in June."

The clerk shuffled papers. "Don't ask me. I only work here. Read the orders."

As Tom read, his head swam: . . . *Proceed by available transportation to Wirtzfeld, Belgium. Report to 394 Regt 2nd Inf Div for assignment.* . . .

"*Second* Division! Corporal, I'm in *106th* Division!"

"Not any more," the clerk said, with a shrug. "It looks like you been transferred."

For four days, chilled and desperate, Tom hitchhiked by truck, ambulance, and jeep across France and Belgium. No one had ever heard of the Golden Lions; few had any knowledge of Wirtzfeld.

Riding in the cab of a truck on the third day, he studied a newspaper map of the winter line, more or less stabilized by snow and mud. Trailing down through the Netherlands, Belgium, Luxembourg, and France, it lodged finally against the French Alps. In eastern Belgium the American front jabbed like a thumb into German territory.

In Liège, Belgium, he was told to get himself to Spa. In Spa, he learned something of what was going on up front, and was directed to Wirtzfeld. He had quit telling people his troubles. In any case, nothing could be done until he reached 2nd Division. But he would have to hit hard when his chance came. For 2nd, he learned from a soldier in a Red Cross canteen, was no place for a new boy to learn the ropes.

He told Tom the division was all messed up in a complicated maneuver with 99th. Though 99th Division controlled the area, 2nd had the task of striking through its lines at the German-held Roer Valley dams. It was very definitely a combat situation, he said.

Tom gave a shiver. He knew he was not combat-wise by several weeks of training. Surely they would not throw a half-trained eighteen-year-old into the line—but in case the stupid Army got as confused about its combat zones as it was about its hospitals, he had better get himself transferred as fast as possible to his own outfit . . . wherever it might be.

He rode into the village of Wirtzfeld with the driver of a shrapnel-torn ambulance. Wind whistled over the leafless trees and ugly plaster buildings. Tom sat on his mittened hands to keep them warm.

The driver had been telling him, with zest, about a terrible battle in the Monschau Forest, where 2nd Division was attacking toward the Roer dams. The man was full of colorful details. Forests were horrible to fight in, he said. You could not dig a proper foxhole because of rocks and roots, and, even if you did, tree bursts rained shrapnel down on you. Casualties flowed back in endless bloody streams. He had brought out men wounded so badly that— Well, you would not believe it. Yet they were forced to keep attacking, for as long as the Krauts controlled the dams they could drown any assault force in the Roer Valley.

Tom dragged his barracks bags from the ambulance, shaken and sick. "Where do I go now?" he asked, faintly.

"Check in at that green hotel up the street. They'll assign you."

At the hotel, Tom was assigned to Company C, 1st Battalion. A master sergeant told him to go over to the motor pool after he got something to eat—just crawl into a truck, he said, they were all going to the same place: the woods near the village of Wahlerscheid. The Germans were hanging on to that town as though it were Berlin itself.

Tom crawled into a truck with some other soldiers. An inch of white ice glazed the truck bed. They spread overcoats on the ice, sat down, and swayed together as the truck lunged along a road through the dour, broken woods. Other men climbed aboard at dismal checkpoints, a haggard, unshaven company of casuals. The cold crept into Tom's marrow. Artillery thudded in the distance; rippling flashes lit the underside of the clouds. He stared at the refuse of savage ground fighting among the trees—burned-out vehicles, tangled branches, sinister lumps of clothing.

A line of Sherman tanks, snorting like bulls, shouldered the truck aside while they lumbered up the road, then smashed off into the woods. Daylight was fading, with mist blowing and snow crystals in the air.

The truck struggled on over the buckled iron surface of what had been bottomless mud a month ago. It stopped. Wind battered the canvas sides. Near the road an ambulance was parked beside a crude stone house where soldiers with red crosses on their helmets huddled on a bench against the wall. A soldier rose quickly from a log, made the thumb gesture for a ride, and came limping toward the road.

The driver honked his horn. "Get the lead out, Mac!" he yelled.

The man broke into a painful trot. Short and dumpy in a muddy overcoat and overlarge helmet, he resembled some half-human beast of burden. As he handed his rifle up to Tom, the truck lunged ahead. The man managed to scramble inside with Tom's help.

"Damfool acts like he had someplace to go!" he panted. Painfully, he let himself down on the floor.

Tom slid his rifle across the ice to him. "Welcome aboard," he said. The new man wore greasy corporal's stripes. He looked grim and half sick. Between the rim of his helmet and an olive-drab scarf wrapped about his neck were battered, be-whiskered features. He appeared anything but talkative, but Tom resolved to ask some questions. Time was leaking away like blood out of a vein. The flash and bang of shells grew closer every time they rounded a turn.

"Where's 1st Battalion area, Corporal?" he asked.

"You mean Red, boy. Up ahead."

"How will I know when—"

"The truck'll stop."

"Oh. —My name's Croft," Tom said, offering his hand.

"Roy Collins," growled the corporal, ignoring it. He twisted to stare at the truck driver. "Is that eight ball going to stay on the road?"

"Why not?"

"Because we'll get shelled if he does. The Kraut artillery's been registered on these roads since 1939."

Tom did not see how the driver could avoid staying on the road. But the corporal was now studying Tom's shoulder patch.

"Hungry an' Sick Division, eh?" He showed his yellowed teeth in a grin.

Tom grinned. "Wait'll we get our growth," he said gamely.

"What are you doing up here? They're way the hell and gone down the line in the Schnee Eifel."

"I got messed up in the hospital. When I came out, they sent me to 2nd by accident."

"You hope!" The corporal reclined his head against the side of the truck. Tom was surprised to see a drowsy smile on his face. "That Schnee Eifel deal was my kind of war, boy. We were down there till last week. Your outfit relieved us to come up here and get our tails shot off."

Hope lifted Tom. "How far south was this?" he asked.

"Hard to say. Anyway, we'd pushed so far ahead of the people on our flanks that they let us dig in for the winter. Just patrol activity. We had these winterized huts and bunkers. My squad even had a little heat stove!"

"That's nothing," said a Negro sergeant with a submachine gun on his lap. *"We* were billeted in a town!"

Tom trembled with excitement. "Listen, Corporal—how

far—" But the corporal was sunk in drowsy remembrance of better times. His eyes closed. He could not even speak, it seemed. Presently the Negro replied:

"Maybe twenty miles, son. The Schnee Eifel's what they call the mountains below the Losheim Gap, south of here. All these mountains are part of the same chain. We came up here in a day. But, man, what a change!"

Roy Collins painfully stretched his legs across the icy floor. Somberly he contemplated his feet. "Know what's good for trench foot, Croft? Two aspirin and a pair of dry socks. At least that's what they gave me at the aid station. So it must be good."

Tom winced as he pictured the feet inside the muddy shoes—purplish, pulpy, excruciatingly tender. "I dried mine on bivouac with heat tablets," he said. "Listen, Corporal, how do you go about seeing the chaplain?"

"Just go over to his dugout. I'll show you where it is when we reach Battalion. What do you want—a Bible?" He grinned.

"I've got to talk to somebody about a transfer—"

"Dream on, brother." Suddenly he flopped on the floor, clawing at the ice. *"Here she comes!"* he yelled.

All the other men were sprawling on the floor, bawling hoarsely at each other. Tom sat there, startled. Then a long, wild scream drilled down through the trees at the truck, rising as though a locomotive were falling from the clouds with its whistle tied down. In the cab, a soldier riding with the driver screamed, *"Get this thing off the road!"*

There was a flash, followed by a jolting, deafening crash. The concussion tore Tom's helmet off. Shrapnel pinged against the side of the truck. Tom threw himself on top of Collins as another shell hurtled in with an earsplitting shriek close beside the road. Shrapnel ripped the truck's canvas sides. The truck went bucking off into the brush. A third shell landed with a flash and a bursting roar, hurling earth and steel in all directions.

Howling in low gear, the truck smashed along a path through the trees. The shelling fell behind. Presently men began sitting up, a couple of them laughing almost hysterically about the closeness of it. Every man's eyes were wide and wild with excitement.

Tom sat up shakily, trying to believe that what people said was true: The war would be over before Christmas. But nothing he had heard in the Monschau Forest so far had sounded remotely like sleigh bells.

The truck pulled into the battalion area, a crowded clearing in the woods. From the hills all about resounded distant explosions—the heavy thud of artillery and the rattle of small-arms fire. Telephone wires slanted into dugouts and bunkers. In a cold and windy dusk, men trudged past galvanized garbage cans from which cooks ladled food into mess kits. Collins told Tom to dump his gear by a fallen log, and they got in a chow line. A cook gave each a dipper of ration crackers softened into mush with hot water. Tom frowned at the concoction as they walked back to the log.

"This is it?"

"That's it, Junior."

Collins sliced half-frozen stew from a C ration into the mush. Tom sliced some hash into it. It tasted as bad as it looked. He chewed lemon drops while Collins smoked a cigarette. Sunken-eyed soldiers in greasy clothing shuffled by.

Flipping his cigarette butt aside, Collins rose with a groan and limped toward the cans of steaming dishwater, his rifle slung over his shoulder. Tom got in line behind him. Collins glanced back in exasperation.

"Get your rifle! Don't you know nothing at all? These woods is crawling with Krauts."

Afterward, he pointed out a blue-and-white flag fluttering on a stick above a dugout. "That's the chaplain's dugout."

". . . Why don't you wait till I see him?" Tom suggested. "Maybe I can go up to the company area with you."

"Nah, I gotta get moving. On these feet it'll take me an hour. I don't want to get caught out after dark. —What's your MOS?" Collins asked.

"Huh? Oh—automatic rifle. Maybe I'll be in your automatic rifle team!" Tom grinned wryly.

"Already up to strength—me and Pete Kelly and our ammunition bearer. Check at the ammo dump when you're ready to leave. There's always a detail going out."

"With any luck," Tom said, "I'll be going back to Wirtzfeld tomorrow."

"That wouldn't be luck—that'd be a miracle. Line outfits don't let go a man till he's plumb wrung out."

"Yes, but there's this regulation about twins. . . ." Tom said.

"Twins?" Collins frowned.

Suddenly Tom was telling him about twins. About Andy. About AR Something-or-other.

"I don't know the number for sure, but the regulation is based on the fact that twins are so close—"

"Lemme tell you about *close*," interrupted Collins, brutally changing the subject. "This assistant gunner of mine, Pete Kelly—him and me work together so close, when he's got a headache I take the aspirin!"

"Take one for me right now," Tom said ruefully.

Collins laughed and whacked him on the back.

A middle-aged man with silver crosses on his lapels

emerged from the chaplain's dugout when Tom sent word in. His skin was gray with fatigue. "What's the problem?" he asked.

While Tom recited his story, the chaplain tested the whisker stubble on his jaws with the backs of his knuckles. "You enlisted, then? —weren't drafted?"

"No, sir. We'd have been drafted anyway, but we enlisted to get it over with."

The chaplain pulled his collar up, and shivered. He looked sick, his eyes glittering with fever, his lips dry. "I'm going down to Spa tomorrow," he said. "I'll speak to someone."

"Thanks very much, Chaplain. It's Croft—C-r-o-f-t."

The chaplain nodded vaguely and went inside. Nice try, Tom thought, hurrying off to the supply dump. He spoke to some men burdened with garlands of machine-gun ammunition.

"C Company?"

One of them looked at him. "Yeah. Carry some of these, Mac."

He let them drape some bandoliers about his neck. The cold weight of the brass and lead, added to that of his gear, almost buckled his knees. They trudged along a dark aisle through the trees. A thin rain had started to blow. His feet were wet and numb. His sore foot throbbed. The detail pulled up beside a tree to which a strip of yellow tape had been tied.

"You said D Company, didn't you?" said the man to whom Tom had spoken.

"No! I said *C!*"

"Oh. Well, we're Dog Company, Mac. If you'd said Charlie Company, I'd 'a' got it. Wise up. Go down the trail and ast somebody."

He took the bandoliers from Tom's neck. "You crumbs!" Tom yelled after him. "You *knew* I said—"

His anger drained away, leaving him cold and frightened. He stumbled down the trail. In the bitter dusk he caught glimpses of gravelike slit trenches half full of freezing water. A voice called from the shadows.

"Where you goin' now, boy?" —A helmeted bundle of winter clothing that spoke with Roy Collins's voice. Tom faced him, giddy with relief.

"Roy! Gosh, I'm lost! Some guys were supposed to be guiding me, but they turned out to be going to D—I mean Dog. —What are you doing?"

Collins got up heavily. "Resting my damn' feet. Carry my pack, will you? Don't think I'm going to make it. We gotta be in the company area before dark."

Tom managed to get the huge load onto his back. He felt like a pack mule. Collins led off, limping more all the time. A few minutes later they walked into the company area, a dreary congregation of foxholes, downed trees, and scattered supplies. Wet and disconsolate men moved around. Collins introduced Tom to a burly staff sergeant standing near a dugout with another noncom. In his heavy winter jacket the sergeant looked topheavy.

"Did they fix you up?" he asked Collins, with a grin.

"Oh, sure. You bet. Fixed me up good."

The sergeant looked at Tom. He had a swarthy face with a hook nose, pale eyes, and a tiny mouth like a hyphen.

"Who's this?"

"Replacement. They attached him to Charlie Company. He came up with me. —This is Sergeant Arabian," Collins told Tom.

Arabian extended his hand. "Let's see your orders."

Tom handed him the damp fold of mimeograph papers. He read them while jabbing at the spaces between his teeth with a toothpick. "BAR man, huh? Good. He'll be on your team, Collins. Your new ammo bearer took sick today."

"Oh, mother! This guy ain't even finished his training. —How much BAR training you had?" he asked Tom.

"Well, I—I'd really just—"

"Okay. I get the picture." Collins glanced in sudden suspicion across the clearing. "They're moving the CP! Ain't we still in reserve?"

The sergeant's tiny mouth puckered. "Now, you know nobody can fight this war but us, Collins. Baker Company came apart. We relieve them in the morning."

Tom stood there feeling cold and emptied out.

"Where's the air force?" Collins argued. "Why can't they soften them up?"

"Bad weather, foolish. Show Croft where to dump his extra gear. Then move out."

Complaining hopelessly, Collins led Tom to a supply point, where he was told to roll a light combat pack. Everything else would be held for him. He began shivering uncontrollably, like the man they were readying for an amputation the morning he left. It was so stupid! He wasn't ready!

They walked to where a huge fir, felled by explosives, lay like a centipede on the stubs of its branches. A man rose from a slit trench beneath it. Gaunt and unshaven, he had knobby cheekbones and a backwoods look. He seemed to be chewing a cud of tobacco.

"Looks like you didn't get sent back to Paris after all, Roy."

Collins cursed the medical department while crawling into the trench. "This is our new man," he growled. "Tom Croft."

Kelly gave Tom a friendly smile. "You better crawl in here, Tom," he said. "The ground's too froze to dig a foxhole, and we're due for a shelling pretty quick."

Tom crawled into the trench. On each side was a narrow ledge a man could lie on or kneel on to fire. Kelly watched him unroll his pack on one of the firing steps.

"Kin you write, Tom?"

Tom tore open a packet of heat tablets. "Write what?"

"Anything."

"I'm not illiterate, if that's what you mean. Just ignorant."

"You done got yourself a job, then. Our ammo bearer was going to write letters home for me, but he taken sick before I could train him. Me, I'm ignorant *and* illiterate." He grinned, showing dark spaces between long teeth.

Embarrassed, Tom realized Kelly had been serious. "Sure, I'll help you," he murmured.

Firing had fallen off to irritable roars here and there. Tom removed his wet footwear, ignited the waxy heat tablets, and shook them around inside his shoes. The trench filled with bitter fumes; soon his shoes were steaming. He drew on dry socks and stuffed the wet ones inside his undershirt. In a short while he was wearing warm, nearly dry shoes and clean socks. The others were astonished.

"Where'd you learn that?" Collins asked, lying on the ledge.

"Back home. My brother and I belonged to a sort of hiking club called the Sierra Club. You've got to rub your feet when you can, and keep them dry. Put your socks inside your underwear and little by little they'll dry out."

"Little by little," Collins murmured drowsily, "you begin to sound useful."

A flare burst above the trees. Chalky pink light flooded the woods. There was a terrifying shriek of 88 shells from the skies, then a series of screams and crashes all around. Shells rocked the forest and showered them with dirt. Sulfurous powdersmoke drifted through the trees. Collins and his buddy discussed, in gasps, whether the Germans were building up to a night attack.

Tom huddled in a corner. He felt like a swimmer being swept toward a waterfall. Wistfully, he remembered things like playing basketball, a year ago; warm ski huts in the Sierras; camping at the beach. It seemed impossible that both worlds existed, the old and the new.

Finally the shelling ended. Kelly told the others to get some sleep. He would take the first watch. Tom crouched in his bedroll, thinking of Andy, writing him a letter in his mind:

Well, I'm out of the hospital, Tiger. Think I may be going back to it pretty soon, though, unless a certain sick chaplain comes through with a pardon for me. It better be quick, though, because up here it doesn't seem to matter whether you're twins or not. . . . Hope your luck is better than mine. Has the Mouth made sergeant yet?

CHAPTER FOUR

The Schnee Eifel, Germany
15 December

For four days Sergeant Nava's platoon drew guard duty, patrolled, cleaned weapons, and slept. Cold all the time, wet most of the time, they listened uneasily to the growling of mysterious engines in the German area.

There were other worries. Lieutenant Sizemore failed to get telephones and ammunition for the strongpoint. The men's long-promised overshoes and hot meals never arrived. And while they had carbines and bazookas, they had little ammunition for them.

On watch the fourth afternoon, Andy gazed at the toylike village down on the Ebrach River. It looked quaint and pretty, like an illustration for a child's book—as though everyone in it were scurrying around in leather breeches and mountain climbers' hats making cuckoo clocks. Sergeant Nava came by with a 2nd Squad man two hours before Andy was to go off duty.

"You're relieved, Croft," he said. "Fall out at 1900 for a patrol. That's seven P.M., if you don't know. No letters, no diary."

Andy tensed. "What's up, Sarge?"

"Little night problem. No sweat."

Andy returned to the squad hut, his face chalky. No letters! That was what they said when there was a chance of your being taken prisoner.

The squad assembled in the darkness by the frosty Sherman tank. Wind whipped ice crystals into their faces. Andy envied the tankers, warm, dry, and bulletproof inside their cast-iron cabin. He and the others debated what the night problem meant. Shanks, feigning confidence, said:

"No sweat. Just follow orders. And shut up—here he comes." In all ways, the Mouth bore himself more like their combat-wise sergeant all the time, even to using Nava's lingo.

Sergeant Nava appeared from the night, dark and solid, the delicate wand of his submachine gun above one shoulder. He called them to attention and inspected weapons.

"At ease, men. Now, we're going down the hill and bag us a prisoner. S-2 is finally getting antsy about our reports of an enemy buildup. We're going to bring a Jerry back and interrogate him."

Joe Sam Tuttle nearly dropped his rifle. "Don't know *how* to take a prisoner, Sarge!"

The sergeant began passing out wound tablets and Red Cross packets. "The Krauts have a listening post behind the second stone wall down the hill. Croft and I will go over the wall and bag the man on watch. He may need to interpret for me."

The sergeant handed out extra M-1 clips and hand grenades. The nightmare was acquiring substance.

"The rest of you wait behind the wall till we come back. Step exactly where the man ahead of you steps, and watch out for trip wires. If you catch a toe on one, you'll set off a mine or a flare. Any questions?"

They marched up to the ridge. Standing in the arctic sweep

of the wind, they gazed across the barbed wire. The fields were black, the woods invisible. Nava peeled aside a strand of wire, beckoned the squad through, and led them down the hill.

Behind Andy, Junior Pettis was babbling to himself. Crusts of frozen snow made footing hazardous. They crawled in silence over the first wall and stole on.

Wind whistled in the stones of the second wall. Andy's flesh crawled. Beyond this wall was the German listening post; he had seen cigarette smoke coming from it this afternoon. Nava gestured angrily at the men. *Spread out!* He whispered to Shanks:

"You're in charge till we get back. Croft—when we get close, I'll give you the elbow. Tell him, *'Hände hoch!'* and keep your mouth shut."

Nava put a leg over the wall as the men fanned out. Junior stumbled; Andy held his breath. With a rattling noise, something tore from the earth.

"Trip wire!" Nava yelled, flopping back behind the wall.

Everyone was yelling, falling, running. Andy huddled against the wall, awaiting the blast of a mine, bleating his brother's name. High in the air he heard a whistle, then a *pop*. A brilliant pink light illuminated the field.

On a tiny parachute, a flare swung slowly down.

Three long-coated gray forms wearing coal-scuttle helmets crouched on the ground a hundred feet to the left. Two of them leaped up and ran. One turned to fire a machine pistol. There were little jets of flame and a shocking clamor. Bullets slurped in the snow near Andy. The Germans dived over the wall out of sight. Nava hurled something after them. A flash, the hollow, clumping roar of a grenade. A man cried out. The other ran alone toward the trees.

Everyone was trying to get a rifle on the third man, still

crouching near the wall. Andy tried to fire his rifle, but it was on safety. He worked the safety. Frozen!

Shanks was screaming, *"Get him! Get him!"*

A rifle cracked. A bullet whined off the ground near the German. He sat up, his hands raised. He babbled in fright. Andy listened. "He's trying to surrender!" he yelled.

"Tell him to lay still till the flare goes out," Nava replied.

German words collided in Andy's mind as he tried to translate the command into German. He called to him, and almost to his surprise the German followed instructions and lay down. Junior ran into the darkness up the hill. At last the flare landed in the snow and fizzed out.

The interrogation of the prisoner took place in Lieutenant Sizemore's quarters. The underground hut was fitted with bunks, a stove, a crude desk. Andy and the prisoner sat on a cot.

The prisoner was a great disappointment. He did not look, at first glance, as though he knew much about Nazi grand strategy. He said his name was Eric Haller; he was fifteen years old. Gefreite Haller did not appear very fierce in his baggy gray coat and pants. He wore steel-rimmed spectacles like Andy's. He seemed dazed, sitting on the cot with his arms crossed. For ten minutes he mumbled while Andy translated.

Sergeant Nava suddenly raised his hand. "What's his unit again?"

"Eighteenth Volks Grenadiers."

"There ain't any 18th VG around here."

"Maybe it's new," the lieutenant said.

Andy questioned Eric Haller about the 18th VG. The boy's hands moved like crabs. Yes, it was new. There were many new units in the Schnee Eifel, old ones, too. Tough panzer outfits from the Russian fronts. A company of rifle-men with supporting armor waiting in the woods!

"Waiting for what?" The lieutenant leaned forward.

Eric chewed a fingernail. "For the counteroffensive."

"What counteroffensive?"

Eric began to perspire. He hesitated, then began blurting everything he knew, as if glad to get it off his mind. . . .

A huge war machine was drawn up along a hundred-mile front. From the Roer dams in the north to Luxembourg in the south, division after division awaited the hour to attack. Straw had been spread over the roads to silence the tanks as they moved into line. Ammunition had been carried forward by hand to save truck fuel and hold down the noise. The troops cooked with charcoal so that woodsmoke would not reveal their numbers.

When the German finally stopped talking, the lieutenant, trembling a little, said one word: "When?"

"It has been for several days planned, but things go wrong. Tonight, when you captured me, we were going up to cut the barbed wire. They say there will be a good fog, and in the morning we attack."

The lieutenant jumped up. He shouted into the covered trench connecting the CP with the communications dugout.

"Worden!"

Sam Worden, the communications corporal, hurried in. He was a smart-mouthed kid from Boston, with tight black hair like a fur cap. "Yessir!" he said.

"Connect the telephone in here and get me the battalion Intelligence officer."

Worden carried in the outfit's only telephone. Mile by mile, he argued for connections back through the crazy telephone net between the front line and Schlausenbach. At last he handed the instrument to Lieutenant Sizemore.

Trying to sound very much in command, yet seriously concerned, the lieutenant related the prisoner's story. The corners of his mouth drooped as he listened to the reply.

". . . Well, but you *see*, Lieutenant," he argued, "we've actually *heard* these engine noises ever since we got here! If they should hit us in force, they'd roll us up like a rug. And from here it's straight down the mountain to the paved road below us. Hell, they'd be in Schlausenbach in a couple of hours!"

Doodling, he listened again, with resentment, irritation, then resignation in his face.

"What about some more antitank guns up here, then, sir? . . . I see. Roger. Will do."

He handed the telephone to Corporal Worden. "Send the prisoner back to battalion headquarters in my jeep," he told Nava.

Nava's face was like brown stone. "Shall I double the watch?"

"Put every man in the line and get the ammo moving up."

At 0430, Andy woke Apache, who was sleeping on the floor of the slit trench. The Indian boy scrambled up, rubbing his face vigorously. They had spelled each other all night, two hours on, two hours off. Andy had been unable actually to sleep.

"You're on," Andy said. "I gotta get some sleep."

Apache worked the action of his rifle to make sure it had not frozen up. They had some waxed ration boxes burning in a gallon can for warmth. He mounted the firing step and peered down the hill as Andy lay down, his body thrumming with exhaustion.

"Fog! Man, they could play kick-the-can and we'd never

hear them." A freezing fog had swirled in an hour before, inundating the ridge in a suffocating whiteness.

Andy fell into a sleep like death. He had no sooner dropped off than a brilliant flash woke him. The ground leaped, and a gigantic bursting crash hurled earth in his face. He screamed. A second explosion came; he sprang up, confused, shouting in terror, and rammed his head into the log parapet. Pain flowed like hot wax from the point of impact down over his neck and shoulders.

"Get your helmet on!" Apache yelled. "It's a barrage!"

Someone was crying for help. The big shells banged in at three-second intervals up and down the ridge. Flashes lit the fog; volleys of giant projectiles passed over, searching out rear-area targets.

For fifteen minutes they crouched in the trench. Each shell arrived with a deafening scream—a crack—an enormous flash—then a whistling of steel fragments. Sometimes a small avalanche of earth rained upon them.

At last there was a lull. The sergeant crawled up beside their trench. In the east, a gray light silhouetted a range of hills. The fog was lifting.

"Everybody okay?" he asked.

They were shaking uncontrollably but unharmed. "Yeah! What's—"

"There's going to be an attack. There'll be some more shelling first. As soon as it's light, watch for tanks and infantry. Here's a tommy gun." He dropped the weapon and some ammunition into the trench.

"What—what do we—"

"Wait till they're close. Don't fire and give away your position. Don't let the noise rattle you. When I give the word to fire, pass it along."

"Sarge—what's the lieutenant say?"

"Nothing. The line's out and the radio's being jammed. But it looks like the big one that Jerry told us about. See those flashes under the clouds? Those are big guns shelling the roads miles back. We may have to pull back, but nobody takes off till I say so."

He ran on.

The shells came roaring in again, screaming and crashing in a vast confusion. Someone was crying. Andy peered out and saw, in a shell flash, a soldier blundering around without rifle or helmet.

"Junior!" he shouted. "Get down!"

Junior disappeared in the smoke and fog.

Shells rained on the backslope and blasted up and down the woods. One of the tanks was ablaze. Suddenly the sky was lit by a brilliant eruption of fireworks. A blast of air struck their faces. They heard a deep, crumpling roar in the woods, and looked back. Streams of firefly-like tracer bullets arched through the sky. There was a series of muffled explosions.

A shell had hit the ammunition dump.

Worden came by carrying a rolled stretcher. His flat, cagey eyes were wide and he was shaking. Moisture dripped from his helmet.

"Who's hit?"

"Don't know—"

Worden started to run on.

"Wait!" Andy called. "What's the lieutenant say?"

"He ain't saying anything, brother. He was getting ammo when the dump went up!"

As abruptly as it had started, the barrage ceased. A ringing silence rolled in, and the sulfurous fumes cleared. Everyone stood on his toes to stare down the hill.

A man screamed, *"Here they come!"*

The tanks emerged from the mist like elephants from a swamp, their gun barrels probing continually, sniffing targets. Then came waves of infantry out of the woods, clambering over the walls, plodding up the hill at quickstep. Some rode the hulls of the tanks. Ramps had been placed over the walls during the night, and the tanks growled up and over them.

A Tiger faltered and swung aside as the gut-shaking explosion of a mine jarred it. Smoke and flame billowed over the hull; one of its tracks fell off. The hatches creaked open, and tankers sprawled out. Another tank lost a track and went into a pinwheel. The infantry faltered.

"Fire!"

Grunting coughs came from the heavy mortars, and machine guns rattled. Suddenly, gray-clad soldiers were falling —a dozen here, half a dozen there, being mowed like wheat in the deadly cones of automatic-weapons fire.

More excited than frightened now, Andy fired, yelled, reloaded. The act he had dreaded—firing at a human being— was absorbed in the violent thrill of seeing the enemy thrown back.

The tanks came into a frontal line. Without warning, searchlights blazed on their bows, blinding the crews of the strongpoint's little antitank cannons. The gunners shaded their eyes and blundered about, struggling to aim and fire. But the Tigers were already blasting the ridge. A cannon and its crew were hurled backward down the slope.

The infantry ran forward again.

"Fire! Fire!"

Black mortar bursts tore at the waves of gray overcoats. Machine guns chopped huge holes in the lines. It was impressive and shocking; for a moment Andy could only stare, numbed. The Germans kept coming, like cattle going over a cliff, falling, crawling, walking into the terrible rain of steel.

At last they wavered and went down. A sputtering return fire began.

Tank engines roared again and gears clashed. A change in strategy: the infantry dug in while the tanks pivoted. Now, what? Andy wondered. The tanks headed south, one after the other, flanks bared to the ridge. But there was nothing left to hit them with. Their lights faded, and they vanished into the mist.

"They're going around the hill," Apache said. "Behind us! That's all we need."

The road from the village turned west below Strongpoint Nighthawk. It passed through the hills, then ran north, becoming the paved road to Schlausenbach. Once on the pavement, the tanks would be in the rear of all the strongpoints.

Leo Miles crawled up. "Getcha packs! We're taking off. Assemble at the CP."

Near the command post, now caved in and burning, stood a truck and a weapons carrier. The sergeant motioned the men aboard as they streamed into the woods.

"Roll two blankets each and load up on rations and grenades. —Where's Junior?" he asked.

"He disappeared," Andy said.

"Figures. Pop! You here?"

"Yessir. What do you want me to do?"

"Same as the others."

Andy climbed in. Men were crawling about, grabbing at supplies, wild-eyed and babbling. One man sobbed in frustration as he tried to roll his blankets.

"Look out with them grenades!" Tuttle screamed. Grenades were clattering about like stones. The sergeant climbed in and the truck lurched off.

"Where's the weapons guys?" a man shouted.

"They're covering our retreat," Nava said. "They'll follow in the carrier. Now, listen: those tanks will be heading north on the Schlausenbach road in a half hour. They'll overrun regimental headquarters unless we hold them a while. Worden, weren't you in Combat Engineers?"

"Yo!" Worden called from the shadows.

"Find the explosives. We're going to set a roadblock. You and I and Shanks will mine the bridge where we come out on the road."

"Shanks is dead!" Rotunno said. "I seen him on the hill with his legs shot off."

"The hell I am!" the Mouth snarled from the darkness.

"Croft, Celaya—find some TNT and plastic tape. Tape TNT to some trees on the far side of the bridge and blow them across the road."

He kept talking, making up bazooka teams, machine-gun teams, rifle teams. Still jumpy, the men were settling down. Leo, who had had some training in firing the bazooka, explained to Vito how to load it.

"Sarge?" It was Shanks' voice. "What's going on? I mean, on the level—"

"On the level, guy, I haven't the faintest idea. We couldn't get anything but German band music on our frequencies, and all the telephone lines are out."

"Well, I mean—is it a big action, or—"

"The way I see it," the sergeant said, "they're hitting us because they know we're undermanned, and new. The lieutenant said we're spread over twenty-six miles instead of the normal four or five. The north end of our sector is in the Losheim Gap. The south end is clear down in Luxembourg."

"Are they just trying to take back their own territory?"

"Ask me again tomorrow," Nava said. "I may be able to tell you more about it then. All I can say right now is, this'll do for a big action till a bigger one comes along."

CHAPTER FIVE

Monschau, Germany
15 December

Tom threshed in the entangling web of a nightmare. Somewhere a man was moaning pitifully, like one of the wounded he had seen in the forest; he whimpered in sympathy. He tried to tear his eyelids open, gasping with the effort, but failed. At last he awoke, dazed, his heart hammering with the vividness of the dream. He sat up and gazed about. A helmeted figure in a raincoat, standing on the fire step, nudged him with his boot.

"You're dreamin', boy," said Pete Kelly, Collins's BAR assistant. "Quiet down."

Tom lay back, relieved but shaken. Lying in the damp slit trench, he shivered with the bone-deep misery of cold and stiffness. With horror he recalled the dream. . . . Andy had been driving a tractor along a steep hillside when over it went, pinning him beneath it. Splashed with blood as red and shiny as enamel, he had begged Tom to help him. But Tom couldn't.

A watery dawn brushed the treetops. A massive shadow loomed over the trench—the downed fir that shielded them from tree bursts. The smell of wet earth filled his nose; his mouth tasted like something dead, and his face was stiff with

dirt. Smeared across his mind were memories of yesterday—
the dead men, the wounded crying out to him, the scream
and bang of shells.

Rumbling and bumping, distant artillery began to shake
the Monschau Forest awake. Strings of machine-gun fire
ripped out. Shells fell in the woods with roars like collapsing
houses; his muscles cramped protectively.

Kelly yawned. "Better crawl out," he said. "We'll be relieving Baker Company any minute."

From adjacent entrenchments came muffled clinks, voices,
the fragrance of a breakfast ration being heated. Stifling a
groan, Tom sat up and tried to separate his things from the
muddy rat's nest of gear on the floor.

"After you get a bite to eat," Kelly said, "you can write
that letter for me."

Tom ripped open a ration box. Looking up with puffy
eyes, he asked, "What letter?"

"You know—to my folks. I ain't wrote in a month. The
tablet's under your gas mask."

Tom remembered promising to be Kelly's secretary. How
did the army find these men, buried so deep in hills and forests that they had never even attended school? He chewed the
cold food and stirred powdered coffee into icy water. Using
the gas mask as a desk, he sat cross-legged and told Kelly to
start dictating.

Kelly dictated the dullest letter one could imagine. He felt
pretty good; his ear still ached a little; it was cold. How was
everybody?

"—And kinda finish it up, like," he said.

Tom sensed that it was he, not Kelly, who was expected to
provide sparkle for the letter. He added some phrases that ex-
pressed how he himself felt about being in Germany, about
his homesickness; he read them aloud. Kelly was delighted; he

praised Tom as though he had just written *Huckleberry Finn.*

"That's real good, Tom." He signed his name in capitals. "Wanted to be sure and get it wrote before we moved up," he said, folding the paper. "Had one of them hunches last night."

"Like what?" asked Tom, uneasily.

"Like—you know—this might be Kelly Day."

Corporal Collins yawned and sat up. "Tell me one day you ain't had that hunch," he said. "What time is it?"

"Time you was awake. Here comes the sarge."

The big hook-nosed platoon sergeant walked up and squatted by the log. "Crawl out of there, you guys. We're moving up. Leave everything you don't need. It'll be picked up. Move out till you see the rest of the platoon."

They left the trench carrying light combat packs, weapons, and ammunition. Tom's pulse fluttered. The short walk was punctuated by bursts of small-arms fire close ahead. They came to where twenty or thirty shadowy figures waited in the woods. Noncoms hurried about with supplies, issuing extra clips of ammunition, rations, sulfa tablets, and bandoliers of machine-gun bullets. The men hooked hand grenades on their jackets and filled canteens at a Lyster bag hung from a branch.

Lieutenant Willis, the young platoon leader, arrived and explained the operation.

They were going to relieve B Company, two or three men advancing at a time to prevent the enemy's detecting the switch and catching them in the open. After they were in position, artillery and mortars would lay down a half-hour barrage on their objective: a bare field, a hill, and an apple orchard on the slope of the hill. At the crest of the hill lay the ruins of a crossroads taproom, amounting to nothing but broken walls and heaps of stones.

"But the cellar's still occupied. In two days we've knocked out a dozen machine guns firing from the windows. Either they've got an arsenal and a full company in there or there's a covered trench back to a supply point in the trees. We can't advance on either side till we take the taproom, because we'd be flanked. Any questions?"

"How come we can't get a flame thrower to clean it out?" asked a noncom.

"If we could get close enough to use one, we could knock it out with rockets. And the trees are in the line of fire. The big problem is accurate enemy mortar fire whenever we get close. They've got an observer somewhere adjusting fire for the mortars. —All right, move out," he ordered.

Sergeant Arabian began sending men forward, a team at a time. Baker Company men drifted back, passing in hurried silence and looking absolutely exhausted. There were no 'You'll-be-sorry!' jokes: up here, *everyone* was sorry. Their faces were black with dirt, powder smoke, and whiskers; their sunken eyes had the dead stone stare of statues.

A hand fell on his shoulder. "Take off, Croft." It was Sergeant Arabian.

Tom turned, whispering urgently: "What do I do, Sergeant? I've never been in combat!"

"Collins will tell you."

Tom chewed his lip. An avalanche of things to remember overwhelmed him: Keep your tail down. . . . Pull the grenade pin, wait, throw . . . keep your interval.

"Move out, damn it!" the sergeant snapped, giving him a shove.

Against every normal instinct Tom hurried forward, bent low, equipment clattering, until Collins called from a hole in the earth, "In here, kid!"

Tom squirmed into a foxhole with the other men, and they huddled in the cold mist to wait. An unbearable excitement and anxiety churned in him. Dawn seeped in like light filtering to the bottom of a dirty aquarium; he stole a glance over the parapet. Only a few ranks of trees lay between the hole and a clearing that sloped up to a ridge whose crest was still hidden in mist. The sodden daylight revealed a gigantic trash of broken weapons, overturned fieldpieces, unexploded grenades, helmets, and ration boxes, all scattered over eight or ten uneven acres of ground. Every yard of earth had been kneaded by explosions.

To his right and left, and at the rear, stood solid walls of dark firs. Several hundred yards away, at the far side of the clearing, a rocky hill rose, covered with a shattered orchard. A rectangle of stones crowned the hill, the remains of a structure of some sort. Below and to the left of the orchard lay the blackened hull of a Panther tank. A concrete dome like a mushroom pushed from the earth near the tank: a pillbox.

Kelly, who had been studying his wristwatch, spoke: "Here she goes."

Seconds later, Tom felt a pulse in the earth and heard a far-off boom. Then there was a rumbling in the sky, a soft whirring as a shell arched over; it died abruptly, with a white-hot flash in the apple orchard. For an eye's blink there was silence, then a crash and a crumbling sound of debris falling. Other shells homed in, each arriving with a whistle and a hiss, a flash and a crash. Soon the whole clearing was torn with explosions. The scene seemed to jolt out of focus. Tom was excited and terrified.

Shells from the regiment's big 105's smashed in with measured regularity, smaller rounds from the battalion's mortars falling by the dozen. The tank rocked with hits and near-hits, and the pillbox, struck again and again, flamed briefly each time, but was undamaged. Shells rummaged in the ruins of the taproom, hurling blocks into the air.

Tom's spirits rose faintly. How could anyone remain alive in that smoking rubble of stone? Or in the woods, where shells burst in the treetops and shrapnel slashed down?

Then, as suddenly as it had commenced, the barrage ended. In the watery daylight, smoke drifted off. Sergeant Arabian wriggled up to the foxhole. His face was smeared with mud and his eyes looked large and staring.

"Five minutes!" He started away.

Kelly raised his hand. "Hey, Sarge! We ain't going straight in at that taproom, are we?"

"You got a better idea? That's where the bullets come from."

Kelly rubbed his forehead, looking nervous.

"How come *we* draw the clearing?" Collins complained. "We always get the dirty end of the stick. Why not them 1st Platoon goldbricks for a change?"

"Because we're in better shape than they are. Anyway, look at the cover out there!" the sergeant said with enthusiasm. "There's so many shell holes in that field, it'd take a direct hit to hurt a man."

"It's them direct hits I was warned about," said Kelly.

Tom shuddered with unbearable excitement. There came a sudden whistling from the sky; the BAR men swore and crouched. It grew to a fluttering whir, while the men waited with hunched shoulders; then the whirring died as a light flashed in the trees. An instant later, a flat crash shook the forest, and stones and earth rumbled. Soon, shells were flying in one after the other, whistling softly, landing, exploding with screaming bangs and crashes. Shell-fragments pinged against the trees and hissed in the wet earth. Cordite made Tom's eyes water. His hands were clenched, his whole body locked in a vise of terror.

Collins punched his shoulder. "Get ready. Pick up the ammo. Soon as you see us drop, find a hole and stay low."

Everything Tom had etched on his mind against the hour of need had been scoured away. He could not go out there, a balloon of flesh in a steel bramble patch. He felt he was about to weep or get sick. Collins shoved an ammunition box at him; he pushed his snarling face into Tom's.

"Did you hear me, stupid?"

Tom nodded, not even sure he could get up. Collins turned away and hooked the legs of the rifle bipod over the lip of the foxhole while he studied the clearing. Tom stared at his back and Kelly's as they waited. Whistles blew.

"Let's go!" someone yelled.

Collins's elbow smashed back into Tom's chest. He crawled from the hole with Kelly beside him, yelling in fear and rage. Tom coughed. Golden flowers of phosphorus bloomed in the clearing. Suddenly men were clambering over the broken ground, stumbling toward the orchard and the slope that tilted up to the platoon's objective: the taproom. Mortar shells fell with black bursts. The crashing—the yells—the swelling gunfire—the roaring. The wild force of them smashed Tom's will to jelly.

Collins turned to scream: "Get the lead out! Get up here!"

Tom staggered up. He could not believe it was happening —that after all the training, the conditioning, the exhortations to protect oneself—you ended up being driven like an animal into a field of certain death. No one could possibly leave this field alive.

Tom followed Collins and Kelly until they sprawled into a shell hole, then flopped down near them and wriggled into a depression still hot and sulfurous from a shellburst. Red tracers zipped over his head from C Company's supporting fire. Automatic weapons stuttered on all sides. In the woods to right and left of the clearing he heard the whine and ping of rifle fire and the roar of grenades. Savage fire fights had broken out as the other platoons struggled to displace the enemy on the flanks and keep up with 2nd Platoon's advance.

He raised his head a few inches. The burned-out tank and pillbox were not far ahead; to the right, the bare ground rose to the rows of ruined trees with their arthritic branches. Yelling, 1st Squad was trying to reach the orchard. Suddenly, machine guns winked and rattled in the ruins of the taproom. The squad was brought up cruelly. GI's stumbled and fell. There were cries for help, screams and moans. Lieutenant Willis hurried by, bent low, a runner with a handie-talkie behind him.

Terrible! Terrible! Tom kept thinking.

Sergeant Arabian appeared beside Collins's hole, red-faced with anger. "Get outa there!" he roared. "Keep going till I say dig in! What the hell's wrong with you?"

The team crawled out and floundered on up the slope toward the orchard. Gales of automatic-weapons fire grew on the flanks. Burp guns chattered, high-pitched and rapid: *Brrrrup! Brrrrup! Brrrrup!* The bullets passed with stinging cracks.

A rifleman sat down near Tom, looking dazed. Then he raised his voice in a prolonged cry: "Me-e-edic!" Tom hesitated, staring at the man's leg, mangled at the knee and crimson with blood. Shaken, he ran to another hole and flopped into it.

"You! Get up! Get up!" someone bawled. An officer in a belted overcoat waved a carbine at him.

Tom rose, babbling an explanation the officer ignored as he went dodging forward followed by his runner. Tom searched for Collins, teeth chattering, his eyes wild. Mortar shells banged. He could hear the fragments whining like hornets. At last he saw the officer sprawl behind a bunker.

The sergeant bawled, "Dig in!"

Tom dropped and wriggled into a shell hole. "Roy! Pete!" he called in panic.

"Over here," Collins yelled.

Tom squirmed deeper into the earth. He squeezed his eyes shut and tried to believe it was a nightmare. Bullets plowed the dirt and pebbles pinged against his helmet. It was a nightmare, but he was wide awake.

For a long time the platoon lay pinned down. Mortar rounds dropped continually. At intervals a man would run to a new hole as explosions bracketed him. He could hear the sergeant and lieutenant shouting back and forth, discussing the possibility of getting artillery fire on the taproom. They decided the danger of shorts was too great, and besides they were getting nearly as much fire from the trees on their flanks as from the hilltop.

"What the hell's wrong with them other platoons?" the sergeant complained. "We can't move till they clean out the woods."

"They've run into trouble," the platoon leader reported. "I'm getting too much static to follow it. But Captain Cole says they probably can't advance till we take the hill."

"*There's* support for you," replied Arabian bitterly. "If we could take the damn hill, they wouldn't have to advance."

At last Collins gave a shout. "Sarge! Ain't that Moreno in the orchard?"

". . . By God it is!" the sergeant said, after a moment. "Look at that little grease ant—"

At first, Tom made out nothing but mortar bursts exploding among the trees. Then he saw a soldier lunge up, sprint a few yards, and dive for cover. He lugged a bazooka under his arm. A second man, laden with ammunition, appeared briefly as he followed. On the hilltop, the automatic weapons burst out with an angry staccato. Wood chips flew from the trees where the GI's had vanished. Somehow the team had worked far up into the orchard without being discovered. If they could crawl another hundred feet, Tom thought, they could blast a couple of rockets into the taproom and knock out the machine-gun nest.

"Get some fire on that taproom!" the sergeant shouted.

Tom squirmed around and took aim on the smoking pile of stones. The embrasure-like windows would have gone unnoticed without the winking muzzles of guns to betray them. He heard M-1's cracking and BAR's rattling. Puffs of rock dust flew around the windows. He fired several shots with no idea of whether his slugs flew high or low, but the volume of fire momentarily bullied the gunners into silence.

The Mexican and his loader sprang up, ran past a tree, and Moreno pitched into a depression. At the lip of it the loader faltered. From the left, a German machine gun ripped out a long, clattering string of fire. The loader reached a hand toward Moreno; another string of shots seemed to chop his legs from beneath him. He fell and rolled over onto his back.

"Where the hell's that gun firing from?" the sergeant shouted. He sounded angry and bewildered. The shooting had come from less than fifty yards away, somewhere between the squad and the woods on the left.

Anxiously, Tom peered over the field. It seemed impossible that a German could have come from the trees, unnoticed, and set up a machine gun in a shell hole. He studied the pillbox. So many shells had exploded against the embrasures, hurling fire and shrapnel inside, that no one could possibly be alive in it. The Panther looked equally dead; everything combustible, including paint, had long since been consumed. But a movement in a bow plate made him look more closely at the blackened hull. A bulging machine-gun port was bolted to the armor like a slotted turtle shell, the gun barrel protruding only a few inches. As he stared, the muzzle seemed to move slightly. The tank had been rolling toward the orchard when it was hit; now the gun trembled and a string of bullets flashed away, arching into the trees.

Tom yelled, pointing. "There's a gunner in that tank!"

Sergeant Arabian raised his head. "Where? There can't be—" But a moment later the gunner cut loose with another burst, and the sergeant shouted for fire on the tank. Rifles and automatic weapons hammered at it. Somehow, during the night, a German had entered the tank. The gun continued firing. The lieutenant called for mortar fire, and high explosive rounds detonated around the squarish hull. But even direct hits could not penetrate the tough steel hide, and there was no fuel, no ammunition rack, to ignite.

The platoon hammered away at the tank, aware, now, that the gunner was probably also adjusting fire for the mortars in the woods. A sense of frustration took hold of the men in the field. In the orchard, the bazookaman had been nailed down by mortar and machine-gun fire. Teams of aid men crawled forward to drag away the most seriously wounded. Most of Tom's M-1 ammunition was gone. Kelly's BAR clips must be nearly empty. And still the lone gunner in the tank held up the platoon's advance.

Lieutenant Willis called to the sergeant.

"His turret hatch is jammed partway open. If we can get in close enough, we can drop a grenade into that tank."

We, Tom thought.

The sergeant raised his head briefly, and Tom saw his dirty face turned toward him. "Croft!" Tom leaped, then lay still, pretending he was wounded . . . he hadn't heard . . . he was dead.

"—Relieve Kelly. Kelly, we'll cover you while you move in. Work around to the left—he can't traverse far enough to hit you. The hatch is open on that side."

"Yo!" Kelly called back.

With a shameful feeling of relief, Tom collected his steel boxes and crawled forward. The earth quivered with the *plip-plip-plip!* of machine-gun bullets near him. He rolled into an anthill-like hole with the BAR men. Kelly was methodically unhooking grenades from his belt. Collins pushed his own grenades at him, and the Southerner stuffed them in his over-coat pockets. Collins looked at Tom, his face yellow, brown smears under his eyes.

"Get in place and keep the clips coming. We'll pin that Kraut down till Pete's up close."

Tom pulled the lid off an ammunition case. Kelly whistled, and the sergeant signaled for covering fire. Collins ripped off an earsplitting string of shots. All the guns were firing as Kelly lurched from the hole. Collins yelled, pouring bullets at the tank until the barrel of the BAR shimmered blue. Tom shoved the clips at Collins as the empties fell. On the crest of the hill, the hidden guns stuttered. Their tracers arched down the slope. The tank gunner tried to follow Kelly as he worked left out of range.

Kelly rolled into a crater.

For a moment the enemy fire dwindled. Kelly rose, lobbed

a grenade at the Panther, and dropped back. The grenade clanged off the hull and exploded on the ground. Kelly waited a moment and hurled another grenade. Like the first, it missed the hatch openings and detonated on the ground.

"You got to get closer!" Collins shouted.

Kelly charged again, his arm cocked to throw another grenade. An explosion shook the ground. The earth lifted under Kelly, breaking and rising with a core of fire at its center. Kelly soared horizontally, like a man on a trampoline. He fell back and lay on the edge of the crater. Bullets chopped at him for a few moments; then a dull quiet followed. Kelly had stepped on a mine.

It had been Kelly Day, after all.

For a half hour, 2nd Platoon moved from hole to hole evading bracketing mortar shells, spending its ammunition and blood in hopeless feints and rushes. In the orchard, Moreno fired some rockets at the taproom. Both rounds smashed into trees; the range was too great for a crude weapon like a rocket launcher. The mortars kept after him like buzzards, and he crawled, dodged, and squirmed among the trees.

At last Lieutenant Willis called out: "Ready to pull back. They're pulling back on the flanks. The Krauts'll murder us."

As the smoke shells laid down a screen, Tom collected gear and glanced uneasily from time to time at the corporal. "Roy. We're pulling back," he said, finally.

Collins had lain with his cheek against the earth ever since the last time they moved. Tom saw him nod and grip the automatic rifle, ready to move. Shortly afterward, through a harsh chemical fog, the survivors of 2nd Platoon crawled back to the woods.

Darkness fell, and a cold fog salted with snow crystals swirled through the broken firs. Artillery crumpled in the distance. For an hour now, Collins, with set lips, had painstakingly cleaned the BAR, running patches through the barrel, rubbing the heat-tarnished frame with an oily rag. Tom slumped on the floor of the slit trench, his heart thudding, too dazed even to try to talk.

At 2130 the sergeant came to pass the word that Charlie Company was going into reserve again. Second Platoon had taken eighteen casualties. On the flanks, the other rifle platoons had suffered losses nearly as heavy. The men silently collected gear for the move to the rest area. As Collins sat waiting, Tom noticed that the side of his neck was black with blood below the ear.

"You're cut, Roy," he said.

Collins touched his neck, looked at the blood on his hand, and wiped it on his pants.

"You'd better go back to the aid station," Tom said. "The cut's pretty close to the vein."

Collins showed interest, probing around the wound.

"They got Pete out all right," Tom said. "I saw them bring him out."

A man from another foxhole paused beside the trench. Unshaven, with a white young face and dented helmet, he looked like a specter. "Movin' back," he said.

They trudged through the freezing mist. By twos and threes the platoon collected in a chilly ravine, and waited, half frozen, until the lieutenant led them on to the company area. The clearing was thronged with silent men carrying crates and weapons toward the rear. The whole unit was on the move, silent and somber.

Sergeant Arabian, smelling of liquor, handed Tom a damp, folded paper.

"Transfer orders, Croft. Wisht I had your connections."

Tom fingered the paper. "Transfer? Where to?" It struck him that perhaps he, as a fresh replacement, might be shifted to whatever company was taking Charlie Company's place!

"You had a request in, didn't you? The chaplain pulled it off for you. You're going down to the 106th area."

Tom's knees almost caved under him. He stared at Arabian. The unreality of the whole terrible day made it hard now to react in any way. "When do I leave?" he asked.

"Right now!" the sergeant replied. "If you ain't with us, by God you ain't going to be using up our supplies. Go back to Battalion tonight and line up a ride."

A thrill rose through Tom like a bubble. He was going back to Andy—back to his own outfit! Away from this sour, devastated forest to the snowy rest area of the Golden Lions.

"The rest of your gear's at the CP. Get somebody to show you," the sergeant growled.

"I'll show him," Collins spoke up. "I got to go to the aid station again."

"You do and you're on report," Arabian snapped.

Collins twisted his head. "Look at this thing on my neck. There's a piece of shrapnel under the skin."

The sergeant turned him to a reflected glow from the clouds. He dabbed away some blood with a bandage, and gave a sardonic chuckle. "Don't turn your head, boy, or you might cut your throat. And don't ever say you ain't a lucky so-and-so. Okay, take off."

For an hour they blundered along trails heaped with branches and battle trash. At some places the litter and mud made it almost impossible to go any farther. Suddenly, however, they were approaching a stone barn with a blackout blanket over the door and gleams of light at the eaves. He heard voices—excited conversation, groans, a man chattering wildly.

"No, it's okay! I'm all right. It's okay!" The man laughed hysterically.

A row of wounded sat on a bench outside the doorway, their bandages luminous in the dark. They shifted their feet for warmth, shuddering with shock and cold. Others lay on stretchers. Collins sat on the bench to wait.

"Wait till I come out," he muttered. "I may need some help."

Tom hesitated, wanting to find the motor pool and get his ride lined up. He saw no way he could help, but he owed it to Collins to wait. In a moment, however, bliss began to flood him. He was going back to his own bunch! Suddenly he was shivering and happy.

Collins emerged with a bandage on his neck. He showed Tom a piece of ragged steel like a flattened pea.

"How about that? It was laying right against my jugular vein."

"You were lucky. Listen, Roy," Tom said, "I—"

Collins shot him a look. "I'll take you over to the motor pool."

As they plodded along, stumbling against each other with exhaustion, he began to mumble like a zombie.

"For every man that sees action, there's twenty that never gets closer to it than Paris. Ain't that a bitch?"

Tom grunted. Ahead, he saw faint gleams of light—reflections on the trucks of the motor pool.

"Guys setting on their cans peckin' at typewriters, making up laundry lists. Goldbricks in Liège and Paris shining officers' shoes. And there's at least five thousand doughs in Paris on forged passes."

"They get the firing squad, though, when they come back."
At last Tom had caught the drift.

"Nobody's been shot for desertion since the Civil War.
And that's a fact."

"But what happens when you want to come back?"

"I'll check into a repple-depple for reassignment. Tell 'em I
got lost—they don't care, long as you come back."

From his pocket he pulled a crumpled paper tag. "Figured
I needed this more than that dead dogface in the aid station,"
he whispered. "I'll make some changes in it and tell the MP's
I'm heading for a field hospital. We might as well travel together. If there's any question, you can back me up."

Tom chewed his lip. Team play, Scout's honor, and the
code of the deserter; a month ago he would have lectured
Collins on cowardice and duty to country. Now he under-
stood perfectly. Collins had gone the route from Normandy
to Germany. A week of days like yesterday, he thought, and
they'd have to burn the woods and sift the ashes to find me.
"Okay," he muttered.

Collins punched his shoulder. "Attaboy. Let's line up a
ride and sack in."

They found a truck, arranged a ride to Honsfeld, and
crawled in the back to sleep. With the wind battering the canvas sides, they spread their sleeping bags. The ruby spark of
Collins's cigarette glowed on and off.

When Tom closed his eyes, he had an unpleasant feeling of
being pulled over backward in a barber chair. He was dizzy
and clammy, and despite his exhaustion lay awake for a long
time.

The next thing he knew, the truck was bouncing over
frozen ruts. In the arched opening at the rear of the truck,

black trees stood against a lead-gray sky. He lay there in his sleeping bag, still drowsy, full of the deepest contentment he had ever known. Distant thunder rolled; flashes lit the sagging clouds. He looked at Collins.

"Storm coming up."

Collins propped himself on one elbow. "That's artillery, buddy. Look at them flashes! Something going on south of here."

Uneasily, Tom continued to study the dark sky, which pulsed like a fluorescent tube trying to light up. His sense of well-being drained away. South! That was the 106th's sector. No, Collins was wrong. The division would never have been shoved into a combat area. Collins was wrong.

PART THREE

The Roadblock War

Between St. Vith and the enemy, there now lay nothing but the wandering remnants of the Golden Lions. Two of the division's three regiments had been surrounded and captured; eight thousand dazed soldiers staggered back to prison camps in lines miles long—next to Bataan, the greatest mass surrender of Americans in history.

The surviving regiment, abandoning most of its equipment, retreated in disorder to the west.

But out of that disorder a new kind of war was growing: a roadblock war. A squad blew a bridge here; a platoon set a successful roadblock there; a lone soldier with a bazooka stalled an armored regiment on a narrow mountain road by crippling the lead tank.

The nature of the battle was becoming clear to frustrated Nazi leaders: a struggle for roads and bridges, in places so tight that a squad could function as effectively as a company. The woods were full of dazed GI's fleeing the enemy, while creating the greatest possible havoc with what weapons they possessed.

CHAPTER SIX

The Schnee Eifel, Germany
16 December

In the Schnee Eifel it was now past 0800. Over the woolly ridges of the mountain chain the milk-white fog had lifted slightly. Lunging and swaying, the truck carrying the survivors of Strongpoint Dragonfly slowed on a steep hillside; the driver kinked the wheel to the right and set the brake.

Sergeant Nava dropped over the tailgate. "Pile out." White-faced and jittery, the men swarmed after him. Andy listened for the sound of tank engines, but heard only the stuttering bark of the truck's exhaust and a moan of wind combing the treetops.

"All right, get the equipment out," the sergeant ordered.

Below them, Andy saw a narrow road glazed with old snow—the Schlausenbach highway. Big firs grew to the edge of it. A hundred feet south, the road crossed a deep and narrow ravine by an ancient stone bridge that had somehow escaped demolition when the area was torn from the Germans.

While the men grappled supplies, an engine sound suddenly came up. Nava gestured the squad out of sight. He got behind a mossy rock with his submachine gun, and they waited. Andy's whole body was weak and cold; yet he felt sweat plastering his undershirt to his skin.

A weapons carrier with the American white star appeared. Crammed into the big boatlike vehicle were the remnants of the heavy-weapons squad. Nava flagged the car down.

"What's the word?"

The men were terrified, and two or three wore clumsy bandages. Nava listened grimly to a noncom's report. The Germans had turned their own guns on them before they made it out.

"Park on the road for a takeoff," he said. "Driver, park the truck around the turn, too."

Andy and Apache crossed the bridge carrying their demolition supplies. Nava, Shanks, and another man were already fixing explosives to the ancient stone pillars. Defensive teams dug in above the road. On the far side, men chipped at the frozen mud with bayonets as they fought to bury the mines.

They taped the TNT packets to the red-barked firs and strung wires back to the detonator, then squatted behind a tree. Apache twisted the key. Andy flinched. There was an intense pink-and-blue flash, a roar, bark and splinters flying through the air. Four huge trees toppled, crashing in a monstrous tangle across the road. Could the Tigers climb over it? Andy wondered. From what he had seen a half hour earlier, he was convinced the Tigers could do anything.

They started back across the bridge. Up the hill, Miles, acting as lookout, suddenly bawled the worst news in the world:

"They're coming! Five tanks and a million Krauts in half-tracks!"

Under the bridge, the sergeant shouted: "Head for the truck! Let those mines go. It's too late. We're almost finished here—"

They gathered at the turn near the truck. A clank of track

plates arose. One by one, like elephants in line, five Tigers rolled into view beyond the bridge. Just short of the fallen trees, the lead tank slowed and gears shifted. Then, scarcely slowing, it clawed its way up and over the tangle of branches and tree trunks.

The tank was past the roadblock and rolling cautiously toward the bridge.

At the last second, the sergeant and Shanks clambered into view from the ravine. They ran into the trees. A moment later the bridge trembled; dust sifted from it as the central arch loosened. Then, with a prolonged, avalanching roar, the middle of the bridge dropped from view.

"Hit the ditch!" someone yelled. "It's gonna fire—"

The tank's turret swiveled. It steadied, and Andy seemed for an instant to be looking directly down the cannon barrel. It flashed, and there was a scream, followed by a crack, a blinding flash. A tree exploded into kindling near the crawling men. Someone cried out. No one stopped to see who it was. Shells were suddenly shrieking in and exploding above them. Andy's ears rang. He could hear the whine of shrapnel. They reached the truck. The shells were roaring in the woods between them and the tanks now. The hill made a parapet to shelter them.

They waited anxiously. Shanks and the sergeant did not appear. "Maybe—maybe we better—" Rotunno stammered.

At last they came. Sam Tuttle, an arm around the neck of each, was being carried half conscious between them. His clothing was torn, and blood, dark and thick, soaked the left leg of his trousers. Nava beckoned.

"Help this man aboard. Damn those 88's! Everybody in and let's go—"

Through gusts of wind and sleet, the cars skidded down the narrow cliffside road. The sergeant gave Tuttle a shot from a morphine syrette and prepared to work on his wound. He pulled Tuttle's trousers down to the knees and gloomily contemplated the gash below his hip. Andy caught a glimpse of puckered flesh, silvery-white bone, and bluish meat. His stomach bucked upward.

"Sarge—where we goin'?" Worden stammered.

"To Battalion. We'll get the big picture there and be reassigned."

Nava taped a compress bandage over Tuttle's wound and dressed him again.

The truck slowed and jounced off on a side road. In a few minutes they came to level ground. The driver swung a half-circle in a clearing and halted beside the weapons carrier. Nava jumped out, the others sprawling after him.

They stood gazing numbly at the smoking ruins of Battalion headquarters. Tents, bunkers, supply dumps—everything had been ravaged by artillery. There was no one in sight. Smoke rose from bunkers; heaps of supplies burned with greasy flames. Of the dozen vehicles parked in the trees, two or three looked sound. The rest had been blown apart by shells. The men drew together.

"They got overrun, same as us," someone said hoarsely.

Nava pushed back his helmet. "No. There'd be Krauts here if they'd got overrun. They just got shelled. I ain't panicking, but I figure the division took quite a mauling this morning. We got to get down to Schlausenbach and find out what the hell goes on."

He smashed his helmet down like a football player going back to the game.

"Scrounge up all the ammo and rations you can find. On

the double! Shanks, check that half-track. If it's okay, we'll take it and leave the truck. Weapons men—load Tuttle in the carrier and take off."

While the men rustled supplies, the sergeant and Worden tried to make radio contact. All frequencies were jammed with calls from other American units, all so tangled that nothing could be made of them. Suddenly, from a ridge half a mile away, there was a clamor of machine-gun and rifle fire.

"Shanks, how's that half-track?" Nava shouted.

"Okay! I've got her warming up—"

The men hurled in a few supplies; the driver and another man climbed into the cab, and the others started scrambling in back. Nava's hand closed on Andy's shoulder.

"Have you ever fired the .50 caliber?"

Andy glanced anxiously at the big angular weapon bolted to the roof of the cab. "Not—Not for record."

"It's for record today," Nava said. "Take over."

The half-track ground down the trail to the highway, and clanked north. According to the sergeant's map, it was only a few miles to the regimental town of Schlausenbach. Ice blurred Andy's glasses, and his face was congealing. He pulled his scarf up to his eyes. He was rigid with cold and terror.

They swung through turns, clattered down straightaways. Suddenly everyone looked up. The half-track was slowing. From its bowels came a screeching of hot metal. The engine died with a tortured yowl, and the vehicle stopped.

Nava sprang down. "Out! Bring all you can carry. We're hiking."

Burdened with packs, weapons, and ammunition, they started after him into the woods. After a few minutes, Nava told Shanks to take the point. He waited as the column passed. Andy saw Pop Newcomb leaning against a tree, his pack at his feet. He looked exhausted and apologetic.

"Come on, kids—who's going to carry the mailman's pack?" he panted.

Miles pushed past him. "The mailman, who else?"

Everyone hurried on, fearful of being left. Nava hoisted the old man's pack onto his shoulder. *"Que caráy!* Old men and kids! Why did it have to happen to *you,* Abe?"

Ten minutes later he halted the column.

"Well, those Battalion jokers did one thing right," he sighed. "They put sugar in the gas tanks so the vehicles couldn't be used. According to the map, it's four miles to Schlausenbach. Team Nava's going to make it afoot. Don't come to me with your blisters, 'cause I've got my own. I didn't ask for this bunch of foulups, but I'm going to get you back to the supply room before I ask for a transfer."

In a blowing mist of snow crystals, Team Nava set off cross-country, despising their sergeant, the cold, their fears.

The snow blew itself out; the wind had the teeth of a fox. They went slowly, in a trance of exhaustion. Pop's pack was carried first by one man, then another, working its way down the column. Carrying only his rifle, the old man was barely able to keep up.

They struggled up a last wooded ridge and gazed down on a mountain valley embraced by dark hills, its floor a pattern of farms, haystacks, and stands of trees where the ground was too hilly to plow. A village was caught like a fly in a spiderweb of roads. Traffic sounds rose in a prolonged groan. A solid line of military traffic crept north into the village. The town lay bleak and frozen on the dark landscape, but it was home. Relief lifted them.

"Hey, Sarge!" Miles said, a depraved grin breaking the stolid misery of his face. "I bet there's some beautiful beasts in that burg, huh?"

Nava smiled. "Miles, you better read your training manual on the Belgians. When a Belgian girl isn't pitching hay, she's pulling a plow or eating heavy food."

Leo sighed. "Man! Could I go for a girl like that!"

They trailed down a brushy ravine to the valley. In a freezing wind, they hiked into the squalid town. Rows of tents flapped on a small square. Soldiers hurried back and forth or stood dejectedly watching the traffic creep by. MP's attempted to direct vehicles down this and that narrow side street. The drivers ignored them. No one knew where he was going, but everyone was in a hurry.

A regimental plaque hung above the entrance of a dingy hotel. The upper floor was caved in by shell hits. Nava told them to wait in the square, and dodged through the traffic to the hotel.

After a full hour he returned. Andy had slept most of the time, his head on his pack. The cold of the ground had penetrated his limbs, and he sat there shuddering as the sergeant angrily told them what he had learned.

Nava sat on his pack and massaged his wet stockinged feet. Andy felt a kinship with this querulous command machine, this Neanderthal soldier who had walked from his cave carrying a rifle and counting cadence. His feet hurt: therefore he was human.

"All our company officers and noncoms have dropped out of sight," he reported. "The battalion CP's moved to Roth. That's a couple of miles north of here, and it's getting shelled. So we aren't going to Roth."

"Then how come all the traffic's going that way?" Shanks asked.

"There's a side road this side of Roth. Why in hell don't some officer step out of that hotel and stop this traffic? Why let all our supplies and heavy weapons leak away without a shot fired?"

He winced and rubbed his feet some more.

"They've got a wall map in there full of colored pins. Hell! There weren't even any *pins* at the key spots! And even you guys know you can't fight a war without pins. I'll tell you the truth—nobody knows any more about this than we do."

Andy gazed at the passing trucks, artillery pieces, and jeeps. Someone *had* to know what went on. Didn't they have retreat plans as well as plans of attack? If they let this rout continue, what would be left to set up a defense line with?

"So what do we do?" he asked. "Just bivouac here?"

"A truck's going to pick us up at 0300. We're going to Owv, I think they call it, couple of miles up the road."

Auw: Andy saw the German spelling in his mind. "What's at Auw?" someone asked. Andy saw it as another dreary and terrible place where only the enemy knew what was happening.

"There's a field artillery outfit there that's getting hit by ground troops. All they've got for defense is a few squads of combat engineers. We'll be part of the scratch force to ease the pressure."

Hopelessness and despondency fell on the men.

"It's rough," said the sergeant, "but we'll be in a line at least, and things will steady down during the night. The enemy will have to stop and dig in. By morning we'll have a picture of what's going on."

A line of trucks with an MP jeep at each end pulled up before the square and started honking. Green young officers and noncoms dropped from the trucks and shouted at the aimless groups of soldiers among the tents.

"All you men get over here! On the double!"

Bewildered soldiers moved to the road. They were prodded into the trucks. Team Nava threw their weapons into the darkness of the last truck in the column, and boarded.

The convoy jerked along the Schlausenbach-Roth road for ten minutes, then turned west on a side road. There were woods on the left, a farm bordered with leafless poplars on the right. Suddenly the driver braked and the truck skidded; crates, barrels, and a few men shot forward. There were cries and curses, the boom of a land mine ahead, then the tearing shriek of machine pistols.

The men crawled out of the debris, sprawled onto the road; scrambling up, they snorted like hurt animals.

A jeep at the front had been blown into the ditch, and sinister bits of clothing hung from the branches of a tree. Men ran about screaming, crawled under trucks, hugged the earth. From the trees there was a steady *brrrup! brrrup! brrrup!* of German automatic-weapon fire.

"My God! A roadblock *here?*" Nava groaned.

He ran around organizing the squad, then led them into the woods on the left. Deep in the trees, they moved toward the head of the column. But by the time they were abreast, the shots and screams had dwindled to a popping of rifles and the moans of wounded men. There were German voices calling; a few pistol shots; then quiet.

A wipeout! Andy thought dazedly. The biggest military foulup in history; it had to be. And now he felt more torn loose from Tom, from the whole world, than he ever had. This was disaster, and every man in it was on his own.

Nava made the *follow-me* gesture, and the squad stumbled after him. Ten minutes later he halted on a low hill. Everyone sank down. Below them a small town lay in flames.

"There she goes," the sergeant said.

For the moment they were too tired to care or to relate the loss of the village in any way to themselves. They lay on their backs in a stupor. Even the sergeant seemed finished, out of ideas. He lay silent on his back, clutching his tommy gun. The clouds sagged over the hills; sunset was not far off.

He sat up presently and studied his map.

"We're at the switch line between our division and 99th," he muttered. "Maybe we'll change our luck and try 99th. Honsfeld; hmm . . . It's only a couple of kilometers. Rest and recreation town. That's what we need, huh? Okay! Everybody on his feet!"

They went downhill to a road, Pop walking between two men with his arms around their necks. It was nearly dark when they saw squarish buildings and leafless trees ahead. In a field, the soda-straw barrels of antiaircraft guns sipped at the clouds. They were astonished when an MP stepped from a comic-opera sentry box and asked where they thought they were going.

"Going!" Nava said. "Where the hell do you think we're going? The whole 106th is on the run! It's a breakthrough."

"No kidding!" The MP repressed a grin. "I did hear about some skirmishing in the Losheim Gap today. You guys are new, ain'cha?"

"I'm not new. And I've seen a division put its tail between its legs and run today. Schlausenbach is a madhouse. Auw fell to the Jerries an hour ago."

Sobering, the MP asked, "You sure?"

"If it wasn't for the weather, you'd have heard the shelling."

Still skeptical, the MP scrutinized the tired young faces, then winked and said: "Get some chow into your army at the Red Cross, Sergeant. Then report to somebody."

Nava tapped the MP's arm. "I'll report, copper. And if you were smart, you'd report, too. Because the way things are going, there's going to be a dead MP in your shoes before your watch ends."

Pushed along by the wind, they hurried into the village.

Traffic was lighter, yet even more frantic, than it had been in Schlausenbach. Trucks and fieldpieces roared through on the east-west road, a dark river in full flood. The men in the vehicles looked as though they believed in the war; the GI's roaming the streets appeared happy and content.

How could the brass miss anything as big as a division shot to pieces? Andy wondered.

They found the canteen. Nava told them he would check in somewhere and join them later. The hall was a big clamorous room crowded with long tables. Its smoky warmth enveloped them like a mother's embrace. Hot food! Coffee! Elbow to elbow, they took over a table and devoured plates of beans, frankfurters, and doughnuts. Pop finished before the others, propped his chin in his hands, and watched Rotunno greedily contemplating his third plate of food. He nudged Andy.

"Get a load of that guy. He looks at food like Leo looks at girls."

"Food don't give you any backtalk," Vito muttered, stuffing his mouth.

Nava came back. He ate in silence and refilled his coffee cup. Somewhere he had bummed a cigar. When he had lighted up, he began to talk.

"A major I talked to said there was a little skirmishing in the Gap today. They hit us at the switch line between 99th

Division and our own. A switch line is always bad news. Each division figures it's the other one's responsibility to keep the strip clear of hostiles."

He puffed the cigar, somber and dead tired.

"He said the traffic is just some regrouping, plus a little overexcitement. He had a supply sergeant issue me two pairs of socks for each of you, and we've got permission to billet in any unoccupied structure we can find."

They had seen and suffered too much not to believe the sergeant was serious. Pop raised his head. "Where does a man go on sick call?"

"I'll find out in the morning."

Shanks subdivided bread crumbs with a dirty thumbnail. His long face mourned the death of his gods—the war gods of rules, regulations, and paper losses. The front had melted like wax, and even his sub-gods, the officers, had run. He was left, like all of them, with his rifle, his sore feet, and his bewilderment.

He spoke hoarsely. "All that crap we been through—that was all normal?"

"Not in my old outfit, it wasn't normal. In the morning I'll hunt up somebody else, if the town's still here. Grab some doughnuts and let's go."

Nava passed up a dozen houses and chose, near the western edge of the village, a ruined farmhouse with an undamaged barn. They filed into the barn, rigged a blackout curtain of shelter halves, and built a little fire. The barn, the mangers, the shaggy mound of hay, gave a Biblical look to the barn that somehow comforted Andy's sore heart.

They threw down hay for pallets and washed their feet in water heated in a bucket over the fire. The sergeant, sprinkling powder on the immersion patches many had developed, made them rub their feet vigorously. Then, while they cleaned weapons, he reconnoitred. He came back, cursing the cold.

"There's a field behind the barn and some woods across the field. We'll have to guard the field as well as the road. Two-hour watches, one watch per man. Pop—Rotunno—you're on first watch. Then you can sleep straight through. Stack guns outside so they won't sweat later and freeze up."

Andy stretched out on the hay, drowning in fatigue. The hay was drafty and cold, and he burrowed deeper. Soon he floated into a trancelike state iridescent with memories of childhood. A sort of long-distance hum in his mind roused him. Dimly he saw Tom's face. He tried to open his eyes, but they were glued shut. His brother was trying to tell him something. He heard his voice calling out in anxiety, "Andy! Andy!" He threshed about, but could not waken. The shadow face faded, and he fell into a tormented sleep.

CHAPTER SEVEN

The Losheim Gap, Germany
16 December

The truck carrying Tom and the corporal south to the Schnee Eifel had been parked for an hour on a snowy road bordered by Christmas-tree-like firs, while a line of 2nd Division vehicles crept from a hidden supply point in the woods, crossed the road, and vanished into the woods to the northeast.

It was now 1000. The bombardment that had begun at dawn had lifted. From the Schnee Eifel, a few miles below the Losheim Gap, sounds of big shells still came now and then. Planes circled in the overcast. They stood beside the truck, stamping their feet on the porcelain surface of the frozen snow, and discussed the meaning of the activity.

"It's got to be an attack," said the driver. "Maybe 106th's got something going. If they was to attack down there, it would take pressure off 2nd, up here."

"No," said Collins. "That sector is already so far ahead of its flanks that a couple of platoons of Hitler Youth could cut it off. If anybody's assaulting, it's Adolf."

A knot of distress hardened under Tom's wishbone. He chewed his lip.

"I don't see how the Germans could mount much of an

attack," he said. "I mean, with all the losses they've been taking—"

Both soldiers looked at him. Collins spat. "That's the newspaper war you're fighting, boy," he said. "We're fightin' with bullets, here."

Tom could not believe that things could get so fouled up that a whole division of kids like Andy and Rotunno and the other wet-lipped infantrymen of the Golden Lions would actually find themselves in combat. It would be like shoving a baby's hand in a meat grinder for laughs.

The last of the trucks vanished in the woods. Two MP's in a jeep motioned them on. They drove for a half hour, passing through a demolished landscape of stone huts in soggy fields, slowing finally on a bench above a narrow valley. The valley was a mile south and a few hundred feet below. Its floor was relatively level, but cluttered with sharp little hills.

"That's the Gap," said the driver. "Hey, look! There's some action goin' on down there."

Along a dimly visible road, Tom made out towers of gray and white smoke leaning with the wind.

"You ain't planning to drive clear down to the highway, are you?" Collins asked the driver.

"Not me, brother! We turn west on a logging road."

The gnarled little forest swallowed them again. In the middle of a hairpin turn they came upon an overturned antitank gun and a burning six-by-six truck. The driver braked and fought to control a skid. They stopped, staring at the wreckage.

"Stray shell, you reckon?" asked the driver, hopefully.

"Let's find that logging road!" Collins said grimly.

A dozen soldiers in field-gray overcoats and coal-scuttle helmets ran from the trees below the gun. They hurried into the woods on the right without seeing the truck.

"Holy tomato! Them's *Krauts*!" gasped the driver.

Collins gave the steering wheel a wrench. "Turn around! Get the hell out of here!"

The driver hauled at the wheel. Collins worked the bolt of his M-1. Tom loaded also. Halfway through the turn, something like a white rhinoceros clanked from the trees above them. The boxy turret of a whitewashed German tank swiveled as it crossed the hard snow. The driver babbled hysterically as he rammed the truck into reverse. Tom stamped on the floorboards in terror as Collins yelled at the driver to hurry up.

The truck backed a few yards; with a screech of gearteeth, it bucked forward. It squeezed past the burning truck and howled off down the grade, rattling and shaking on the ruts. Trees ran past the windows; a telephone wire flicked overhead. A shell whistled above and exploded in the woods with a flash. The truck jittered through more turns, roared through straightaways.

The driver swore. "Look yonder!"

A jeep was parked at the edge of the road. Beside it stood a burly figure in an officer's shortcoat and a GI helmet. He semaphored a carbine as they approached. The truck's cold brakes shrilled; it came to a halt, and the officer moved to the driver's side. He was about thirty, short and bull-like, the classic physical type around which football coaches built line plays.

He looked calm, and he was grinning. "Where's the fire— as the saying goes?"

"Sir," chattered the driver, "there's Jerries all over the woods! We can't stop!"

"You just did," the lieutenant said. "How about some gas? A jeep can ought to fix me up good."

"Lieutenant," said Collins, "you'd better survey that jeep

and get in with us. The Jerries are attacking everyplace!"

"I haven't seen any," said the officer. "Come on—gas up my jeep. That's an order."

Tom groaned and jumped out. Clearly the lieutenant thought they had been frightened by imaginary Germans. But he was the officer, and, according to the book, officers had brains where enlisted men had helmets. As they poured fuel into the tank of his jeep, the lieutenant questioned them about what they had seen. Tom caught a whiff of his breath. It smelled like a sour wineskin. He's drunk! he thought, shocked. They finished pouring, while the driver impatiently revved up the engine of the truck.

"Where were you men going so fast?" asked the lieutenant. He had lit a cigarette, and now seemed completely relaxed, prepared to chat a while.

"Honsfeld—*sir*," said Collins, bitterly and with obvious disrespect.

"Watch that stuff," said the officer, with a wink at Tom. "I'd bust you to Pfc., except that I like your face. You've got a real infantryman's face, Corporal. I can tell you're a man to ride the river with. Ever read Zane Grey?"

"No, sir." Collins stood there chewing his lip and dying by inches.

"*Riders of the Purple Sage*—says everything there is to say about the human dilemma. Old Z. G. never put on airs, either. Thoughts of one syllable. Well, don't stand there! Get your gear out of the truck so we can roll."

We! At their stunned expressions, he began to laugh.

"Sir," Tom said, "it's the truth! There's a German attack—"

"I know, I know! Don't panic, soldier. My name's Fox. I lost a patrol in the woods this morning. Now I've got to get back to my command post and pick up some code books and stuff before the Jerries get hold of it. Then I'll take you to Honsfeld. In other words, I'm taking you over."

The driver thrust his head out the window, and shouted, "You guys coming or ain'cha?"

"Wait a minute!" Collins called back. He scrubbed his unshaven jaws with his mitten. "Lieutenant, we're both casualties, see? He's got dysentery, and I got trench foot. All we'd be is liabilities to you."

The lieutenant shed his good humor like a mask. "Get your gear," he ordered.

They hauled their gear from the truck. As they lugged it toward the jeep, the truck howled away down the road. Some day, two years from now, Tom reflected bitterly, I suppose we can protest through channels. But for the time being, the situation was a simple Army one: The lieutenant had given them an order. He could shoot them on the spot for refusing to obey.

As the lieutenant drove on, he wore an expression of drowsy amusement. Once he looked back, then burst out laughing. He was, Tom realized, probably suffering combat fatigue as well as being drunk.

"Come on, relax!" said the lieutenant. "That's another order."

"Where we goin', Lieutenant?" Collins muttered, huddled down under his overcoat and helmet.

The jeep climbed recklessly over logs and boulders on some undiscernible trail the lieutenant seemed to know.

"Well, I'll tell you. I had a platoon of tank destroyers up to 0500 this morning. All we did was to run contact patrols. Yesterday I got nervous about the lousy defense setup I inherited, so I moved. At dawn the biggest shells in Germany began dropping on us. Millions of them! Big as Chevrolets! It went on for a half hour. When the barrage lifted, I was the only man alive, except the patrol I'd sent out. And now I can't even find them."

He kept talking, getting it off his chest.

He would laugh, then become very solemn. He had had basic infantry training, he said, but for some reason he was assigned to division headquarters in St. Vith as a regimental historian.

Suddenly, four days ago, with no training whatsoever, he was ordered into the line to take over a 14th Cavalry outfit.

The jeep burst from a stand of firs onto a stony hillside. Tom and the corporal crowded forward to stare at the pass below them. There were the foothills of the Schnee Eifel on the south, where Tom was supposed to be going. But in between lay the rough little valley called the Losheim Gap; it was smoking and crawling with action. Tanks were parked solid along the highway. Infantrymen hiked beside the tanks. At a railroad overpass, a fierce phosphorous fire burned. The armored column had been stalled by damage to the bridge.

The lieutenant studied the action a while, then drew a long-necked bottle from under his seat. He pulled the cork.

"Calvados," he said. "The fighting man's milk. For Big Combat, you need Big C." He took two long drinks, then pointed with the bottle into the bleak valley below.

"That's the Gap. It'll really louse up my history of the action in the VIII Corps sector if those Tigers get through. They could roll clear to Long Island. I've got chapters written in advance all the way to the capture of the Roer dams by 2nd Division—"

The lieutenant drove down into a tangle of rocks and shattered trees. Equipment was strewn over the frozen mud; there was a smell of burned rubber. A mound of supplies, ripped open like a dead horse, burned greasily. Bodies lay among the rocks, bloody and broken; rags of uniform were caught on the stumps. Tom squeezed his eyes shut until his stomach stopped bunching. The lieutenant gazed sadly at the ruins.

"What I can't understand is why the old defense didn't get shelled, and this one did. What do you think, Corp?"

"The peasants saw you moving and passed the word. You were on the grids before you finished moving. What did you want to get here?"

The lieutenant, collecting himself, sprang out in good style. "I'll find it. You men put the, er, bodies in that slit trench and cover them up the best you can. They were nice kids. Hang their dog tags on their rifles—like you see in the magazines, you know."

They buried seven bodies in the slit trench. The lieutenant unearthed a small steel crate, carried it to the jeep, and ceremoniously loaded it in the rear. He covered it with a shelter half so that it would not be visible.

"There's a patrol coming this way, Lieutenant," Collins reported suddenly.

Lieutenant Fox studied the line of German infantrymen trudging toward the foothills. "I'd like to set up an ambush," he muttered. "But I guess we'd better roll."

The lieutenant drove with flair and imagination. He would ram the jeep between two red-barked firs that Tom would have sworn a bicycle could not get through. Then he would make an elaborate detour when he claimed he heard rifle fire ahead. Fifteen minutes later, however, they would pass the same spot. He was still drinking, but fighting the brandy the way a punch-drunk boxer resists the concept of unconsciousness. It would take a lot of Calvados to put him down for good, Tom decided, but from what he had seen of Army drinkers, he knew the alcohol would finally drop him like a bullet.

The lieutenant bragged that no one, but no one, knew the Ardennes Forest road net as he did. Half his job as historian had been spelling officers' names right, the other half was knowing all the roads.

"After we cross that highway where I shanghaied you guys," he said, "start looking for yellow tapes on trees. There's a logging trail in there that'll take us to the Honsfeld road."

Collins and Tom looked at each other.

"Sir," Tom said, leaning forward, "we're looking for it now. We crossed that road five minutes ago."

The lieutenant braked the jeep suddenly.

"I must be plowed," he said. He killed the engine. They were in a square open space like a small room. The ground was covered with dead ferns, and the darkness of the forest was deep, mysterious, and solemn. With the engine stilled, the far-off clamor of a fire fight came up. It might be a mile away. Big shells whistled overhead to explode in the distance.

Lieutenant Fox fumbled with the radio. A grating of static snarled out at him. Voices floated in and out, excited and unintelligible.

"The firing," he said, "is at Manderfeld. That's Headquarters. Damn. They're encircled. We may have to go down and help them."

Tom and Collins exchanged glances that said, *If he heads that way, we'll jump out.*

But Lieutenant Fox gave up with a sigh. "Bad day at Manderfeld," he said. "Wonderfeld. Wonderful, wonderful, Manderfeld. Say again, Lagoon Red. No can. Hey, whicha you kids— What's your name again?" He smiled murkily at Tom. He was very sleepy now, and his pale square face was sad despite his smile.

Tom sat forward. "Why don't you lie down while one of us drives?"

"Great idea. Crawl outa there, damn you, so I can lie down. Have faith in your officers, men."

They changed places, and he immediately fell asleep. Tom studied the maps. He and Collins agreed on a direction, and Collins started driving.

To their surprise, almost at once they found the yellow tapes nailed to a line of trees. The tapes led them to a highway jammed with traffic. Collins crowded into line.

They traveled for two hours. Though it was only midafternoon, a cold, greenish twilight descended. Tom saw a road sign and stood up to read it.

"Honsfeld! Six kilometers! I'd better try to wake up the general."

A truck loaded with soldiers pulled in ahead of them from the woods at the left. "Leave him alone," Collins said. "By the time he wakes up, you'll be in St. Vith and I'll be on my way to Paris. We'll keep driving till we have to quit."

"What do you figure is going on?"

"German spoiling action. They hit us where we were soft —your Hungry an' Sick Division. First Army will probably send a reserve division in to plug it up tomorrow. Right now, I don't reckon you've got any division to report to."

"We weren't *that* soft," Tom said defensively.

Collins grinned. "Then where's that 422nd truck ahead of us going? Ain't that your regiment?"

Tom studied the markings on the back of the truck. He stood up in excitement and signaled the silent soldiers huddled under the canvas top. They looked at him but paid no attention. He put his hands to his mouth and yelled.

"Hey, Four-two-two! Where you from?"

The soldiers ignored him. They looked miserable and cold. He sat down. "They act pretty stupid."

"They probably seen some action today. You acted kind of stupid last night, too."

"What do you think happened down there?"

"I don't think nothin', Private. I just put one foot in front of the other. Why don't you have a shot of the general's applejack, and relax?"

Tom slumped on the seat, sick with worry. He felt as though his veins had been drained and he had been given a transfusion of tap water. Experimentally, he probed the raw memory of the fighting in the Monschau Forest, relating it to what might have happened to Andy. He winced.

They descended into a mountain meadow where the air was tangy with woodsmoke. It was now almost dark. A village lay ahead, a cutout of blocky buildings and the round, silo-like tower of a church. There was a creaking of springs from the rear seat. Lieutenant Fox had surfaced. He sat up, his face blank.

"Where are we?"

"Honsfeld, sir," Collins said.

"Watch for a headquarters. This is a 99th Division recreational town. What's all the traffic?"

"Refugee. Lieutenant, why don't—"

"Why don't you just drive?"

By some magic of body chemistry, Lieutenant Fox seemed to have thrown off his intoxication and returned to the living, surly and alert.

At the town square, traffic squeezed into a semisolid mass. Horns bleated, engines barked, radiators steamed. On the walks moved a strange pedestrian traffic. The carefree boy soldiers of the 99th Division walked with their arms around Belgian girls. But in the trucks and prime movers there rode the same frightened breed of men as in the jeep.

Now the traffic barely crept along, and Tom twisted quickly.

"Sir, that truck ahead's from my regiment. Can I talk to those men for a minute?"

The lieutenant nodded. Tom paced behind the truck, staring through the tailgate for a face that, by some miracle, he might know. But all the faces were strange to him.

"Whatcha doing up here?" he asked the men.

A sergeant said: "The story goes that we're regrouping."

"What happened?"

"Weren't you there? They came over the mountains like a million screaming apes. We made it back to Bleialf, loaded up, and took off. Got any cigarettes?"

"No. Sorry. What battalion?"

The truck blasted smoke and steam at him; if the sergeant answered he was unable to hear him as it pulled away. The jeep had halted at the walk before a doorway with a headquarters insignia. Climbing out, Lieutenant Fox swayed on the walk for a moment, breathing deeply as he studied the closed door.

"Wait here," he said.

"The next sound you hear," Collins told Tom, as the lieutenant entered the command post, "will be a firing squad."

But in a few minutes the lieutenant emerged with a major with a pink-faced, well-barbered look. Both men were smiling. They gazed at the traffic.

"I'm in no position to criticize," said the major, "since our own men are so green they call us the Battle Babies. But damn it, I wish those 106th people would stay south of the switch line in their own sector! They're getting everyone stirred up."

"So you don't think it's really a breakthrough?"

"There was some fighting in the Losheim Gap this afternoon. No doubt some of it slopped over into the Schnee Eifel sector. That's the way the colonel analyzes it, and I tend to agree with him. Your own experience—well, that was German patrol action, apparently."

"*Very* good," said the lieutenant, as though the whole matter of the assault were now clarified.

"You'll have to go back to St. Vith to reach your headquarters. All the roads around here will be jammed. Take the north road—Büllingen—to Malmédy, then down to St. Vith. You can't miss it."

The lieutenant leaned into the jeep and opened the steel crate. Tom saw the dark shine of a case of liquor bottles. Was that the classified material they had risked their lives to recover? Lieutenant Fox handed the major two bottles of Calvados.

"I picked up a couple of casualties, Major. I wonder if you'd give them a decent burial?"

"With full military honors," said the major, with a grave nod.

Lieutenant Fox leaned against the jeep as the major reentered the headquarters building. He looked at the men in perplexity.

"I felt like the last genius in a world full of idiots in there," he said. "Before I got halfway through my story, they were telling *me* what had happened to my platoon. They've been getting 'scare' reports all day. I was so damn' drunk, maybe I really don't know—What *did* happen?" he asked.

"You got wiped out," Tom said. "And those guys in the

truck said they were overrun too. Lieutenant, *somebody's* got to believe you, if you keep trying!"

"Not in this army. Majors tend to believe colonels—you heard the man. We'll eat and roll. We're going to St. Vith."

"Lieutenant," Tom said quickly, "I've got a twin brother in 422nd Regiment. Did anybody mention what happened down there?"

"No. A twin, eh? Doesn't the Army keep twins together?"

Tom told him about it as they hunted the Red Cross canteen. Fox listened with what seemed to be genuine interest.

He said: "I'll get you kids back together as soon as we reach St. Vith. Build a fire under somebody. That's a crime. Twins are pretty close, eh?"

"Yes. I was worried about my brother, at first—I still am." But now I'm getting kind of worried about me, he thought.

The jeep's blue cat's-eye lamps were no match for the wintry darkness. The lieutenant drove up a steep road from Honsfeld to Büllingen. There was no traffic on the road. As the fierce arctic wind rushed at them, toothed with ice, they huddled wretchedly on the hard seats. Near the top of the hill, an MP halted the vehicle. The lieutenant said they were heading for Malmédy.

"Turn left at the top. No smoking—this here's a fuel dump. What's all the noise in Honsfeld? Sounds like New Year's Eve in a junkyard."

"There was some skirmishing in the Gap today. We heard they're regrouping."

Tom sat up as they moved along a narrow slot between high, fluted walls of stacked fuel barrels under coarse netting —millions of gallons of gasoline and oil. The road forked and they turned west, stole through a tiny village where no life stirred, passed beneath the arches of an ancient overpass, and skidded off the road into the ditch. The lieutenant tried to back out, but it took the two enlisted men to push the car back into the ruts. It was black and windy, and Tom shook with cold. He was beginning to pass into tortured comas of fatigue when the jeep whirled from the road into a farm-yard.

The lieutenant switched on the headlights. "Nobody'll see a light in this weather," he said confidently.

The lights picked out a battered farmhouse, a dead cow with its legs raised like those of a sawhorse, and a barn with one corner torn away and only half the roof remaining.

"That's good enough," he said. "We'll spend the night here."

He sent the jeep lurching over the rubble into the barn. They made pallets from hay and started a fire with hay and boards. Collins was going to flop down as he was, but Tom said: "Rub your feet, Roy. You're going to lose some toes if you don't get the circulation going."

Collins scowled, then glanced at the lieutenant. "Guess you're right. Only reason they pulled me out of the line was my lousy feet. I'm going to the base hospital at Liège for treatment," he told the lieutenant.

Bent over a map he had pinned down with stones, the lieutenant grunted, "You hope."

"I *know*—sir. Here's my evacuation tag."

"And here's our war. By tomorrow they'll have generals carrying rifles and filling sandbags. St. Vith was ten miles behind the front line this morning. It may be in German hands tomorrow. They'll need all of us, Corp."

"Not me. The doctors said—"

"I haven't heard you complaining of pain before, Corp."

"I'm okay long as I stay off them," Collins muttered.

"Well, no sweat. Get some sleep."

Tom drew into his sleeping bag like a snail. He felt lost, cut loose, utterly alone. Now that he was finally on the road, there was nowhere to report. He was almost glad this boozy regimental historian had shanghaied them. For a while, at least, he belonged to some kind of outfit, however small, however crazy.

PART FOUR

The Bridge at Stavelot

The narrow Ardennes roads were glutted with German battle traffic. Commanders fought over the right-of-way while traffic piled up. Hitler's timetable, all-important to success, had to be revised hourly. With precious hours won, Allied units began to swing into position.

Only Colonel Peiper's 1st SS Panzer Regiment, in the north, spearheading the whole drive to the Meuse River crossings, was still roughly on schedule.

Over muddy roads Peiper drove fast, his 142 tanks snorting along behind him. Yet even Peiper saw trouble ahead, as his fuel tanks began to run dry. Then, near Honsfeld, his scouts discovered a large gasoline dump in the hills. Boldly, Peiper left his assigned route to swing his column north toward Honsfeld and refuel on GI gas.

CHAPTER EIGHT

Honsfeld, Belgium
17 December

A hand jarred Andy out of sleep. Nava growled like a dog:
"You're on, Croft—"

Andy's eyelids raised. A dark, whiskered face; the dim in-
terior of a barn. His eyes closed. Like a trout he slipped down
a bank sweetly, and fell asleep.

"I mean *now!*" the sergeant snarled.

With a moan, Andy rolled out of the hay, tired, cold, itchy.
He found his glasses and stumbled to the tiny fire in the corner where canteen cups of coffee waited for him and Worden,
the other guard. The freezing cold crowded right up to the
fire, encircling it like a pack of wolves. The cold thickened
and slowed his thoughts. He picked up the coffee, and shuddered.

"What time is it?" Worden asked Nava. The sergeant was
on one knee, lighting a cigarette in the flames.

"Oh-two-hundred."

Andy reckoned. They would get off at 0400—4:00 A.M.
Two hours of living death. This exhaustion of his was like a
poison.

"Worden, take the post behind the barn. There's a woods

across the field. If you watch long enough, you'll begin to see the trees. Keep watching for anything that moves."

Worden muttered in his scarf, muffled to his nose.

"I'd better post you," Nava told Andy. "There's a hole in the kitchen floor you might fall through."

They crossed the dark frost-glinting yard.

"What am I supposed to do?"

"Watch the road for Krauts. They could march through this idiot town and nobody'd know the difference. If you see any, wake me up. But for Pete's sake don't fire!"

They groped across a dark kitchen to a small, wet-smelling parlor. Miles, seated on a box by a front window, got up and handed his submachine gun to Andy. "The traffic's letting up," he said. "Have a nice watch."

Andy sat on the box as they left. His feet throbbed. He turned up his collar and drew his overcoat sleeves down to cover the bracelets of bare skin left by the idiotically short GI mittens. Remorselessly the wind blew through the broken window. On the road, trucks, a command car, a light tank, passed hastily at intervals. He was drowsing in languor; the stupor of exhaustion swept him in waves. A crash at his feet startled him. He leaped up, his heart pounding.

The gun lay on the floor. It had slipped from his lap, though he had not been aware of having fallen asleep.

He fought the tanglefoot enemy by moving about the floor swinging his arms. Sandy-eyed, he gazed out at the traffic. It had fallen off. A lonely jeep whined past. He sat down, put one shoulder against the wall, and almost immediately felt his head dropping forward, borne down by the heavy helmet. He seduced himself with sweet talk of closing his eyes for just a second . . . kind of coasting . . . just tasting sleep, not swallowing it.

He floated off on the surface of a languor so delicious that he wanted to sail it forever, like a boatman on a misty lake. Again the crash of the gun on the floor woke him. In misery he rocked back and forth, rubbing his chilled face in his mittens. He raised his head, frowning, as he detected a change in the pitch of traffic.

He scrutinized the road. Heavy tanks were snorting along like elephants. An armored personnel carrier hurried past, packed with soldiers whose helmets shone with frost. More tanks rattled and grated along, soldiers crouching on the hulls of some of them. The hugeness of the tanks impressed him, sleepy as he was.

Suddenly he stood up, staring.

The tanks were not Shermans. They had the same square hulls of the King Tigers that had stormed the strongpoint. Andy turned and tripped over a broken footstool; he fell, then crawled through the kitchen to the back door and slipped into the yard. He ran to where Worden was on duty behind the barn.

"German tanks on the road!"

The little signalman jumped in surprise, then pointed across the field. "Look out there! What *are* those things?"

Andy saw a line of wraiths weaving and dancing before the distant trees. "Better come inside!"

Nava, sleeping near the embers of the fire, sat up as he ran into the barn. "What's up? Who's that?" he barked. A pistol sparkled in his hand.

As Andy gasped it out, the sergeant rolled to his feet and went around kicking men awake. "On your feet! Get your shoes on and keep quiet."

Worden slipped into the barn. "Sarge! Hundreds of guys in sheets coming across the field!"

Nava hurried out. The barn was full of dazed men getting under their packs, whispering, dumping coins and pocket objects from their helmets into their hands. Nava reentered with an armload of frosty weapons.

"It's Jerries. Work the bolts of your weapons and make sure they aren't froze up."

"We gonna fight?" Shanks chattered.

"Nossir. We're gonna run. It's dark enough that we may be able to get aboard a tank. They're used to doughs hitching rides. Carry your helmets and wear your OD caps. Pop, what the hell are you doing?"

Pop was seated on the floor wriggling his toes in the glow of the coals. "End of my RFD route, fella," he said. "The mailman joined to post letters, not fight. Just can't go it. I'm gonna surrender."

Nava jammed Pop's helmet down over his cap, then hauled him to his feet. "First place, you'd be shot for not trying to evade capture if you ever got liberated. Second place, you'd die on a prison diet of turnips. Your feet would rot off, your teeth'd fall out—"

"My teeth fell out years ago," Pop said bitterly, "and have you smelled my feet lately?"

The sergeant lined them up at the door and explained the operation. Andy felt feverishly hot, yet he shivered uncontrollably. There was a thicket of second-growth trees just up the road from the farm. They would make their way to the thicket, wait for the right tank, and board it. A couple of miles out of town, they would jump off and head west, since the assault force was now heading north. He did not think it would travel far in that direction before coming back to the main westbound road. A big fuel dump was located at Büllingen, a couple of miles north. He felt that these tanks, which must have come a long way without refueling, planned to capture the Büllingen dump before continuing their drive west.

It was no ordinary assault force, he said. Any regular combat team would now be blasting the defenders of Honsfeld out of their billets instead of bypassing them. This was a hit-and-run battle group, out to seize bridges and highways for the main body of the attacking force that would follow.

They hid shivering in the thicket while German armor shook the earth under them. Andy stared at the passing tanks. Soldiers rode the hulls of some, while others were heaped with supplies lashed down like crates on the deck of a freighter. An all-purpose car pulled up and a man jumped out. He shot the beam of a flashlight at the tank following. It halted; the column stopped. Andy crouched lower.

There was a discussion among several men with maps. The man with the flashlight remounted and drove on. The column pulled ahead again, loosening as slower vehicles fell behind.

"Go!"

Nava stepped into the road. The next tank in line had fallen some distance behind. A King Tiger was pulling by them. The sergeant found handholds and scrambled aboard. Andy followed him, so weak with fear he could scarcely climb. As the tank rocked along, the others boarded in silence and crouched on the broad, flat deck, partially hidden by crates, kegs, and extra tank tracks. Behind them snorted a Panther with dim lights, hurrying to catch up. There was too little light to betray the squad, but dawn was soaking through the clouds.

Nava crawled up to Andy. "If anybody asks anything, answer for us. Double-talk it—act dumb. We'll get off pretty quick and start hiking."

Andy nodded. The tracks beat the road under them, *chunk-*

chunk-chunk-chunk; the exhaust disgorged smoke and steam. The Panther in back nuzzled close to the Tiger's ammunition rack, as if for protection.

A turn in the road bent the column north. Nava kept glancing back. A hatch cover opened and a tanker climbed into view and called out in German. Everyone got ready to jump.

"What's he saying?" Nava whispered.

Andy shook his head. "I—I didn't—*Was ist los?*" he called.

"Low on fuel! Running out!" the tanker shouted.

"Almost there," Andy called back, in German. "Couple of kilometers." And God bless my old German baby-sitter! he thought.

The hatch closed on the tanker.

Now the road tilted, and the tanks shifted gears. The sergeant scrutinized the winter-killed brush beside the road. The blowing clouds tore open, and there was suddenly a leaden look of dawn.

"Ready! We're going over the side."

They dropped to the road and route-stepped along. The Panther grated past. Nava jumped the ditch and smashed into a thicket, the squad scrambling after. Down a ravine they trotted where the cold settled like a refrigerating gas; over a ridge, down another ravine, and onto a hillside where they sank down to rest. There was light enough to take an azimuth, and the sergeant laid his compass on a map and talked to himself.

". . . Hit that westbound road in about a mile, Abe. Moderscheid. Let's see. No—Meyerode! That's good, Abe. That's good." He folded the map. "Up! On your feet, damn it!"

They blundered onto a road that twisted up a hill. Artillery had begun to shake the air like frightened heartbeats. Flashes lit the far hills. Andy saw at once that the morning's fighting was miles behind yesterday's front. At the top of the hill, they halted and gazed out over an arctic landscape of field and forest. Behind them, Honsfeld now lay buried in smoke. Small-arms fire and detonations came from the town.

Honsfeld was falling even as it woke.

"Where's the line, Sergeant?" he asked.

"There isn't any. The Jerries are just grabbing everything in sight. Didn't Abe tell you the Losheim Gap was murder? But nobody'd listen."

They hiked. Andy's swollen feet throbbed. It was not clear to him where they were going. There seemed no safe way now to reach the St. Vith road. Nothing was clear but that the road was steep and everyone was limping, staggering, and groaning. In their pain and anxiety, the men began groaning a little louder, limping more pronouncedly.

The sergeant stepped aside and bellowed: "Now, cut out this bitching and moaning! If you can't march without stumbling, you'll damn well count cadence."

The Lions dragged themselves erect. Andy was resentful, yet obscurely grateful that someone still cared how they marched. The complaining ceased; the intervals tightened. Suddenly, in the quiet following his tirade, the chugging of an automobile engine came from below them.

The squad took cover. The chugging faded, then roared out as a big, clumsy command car burst from some trees and charged up. The markings told them it was American. Five GI's in clean overcoats and helmets huddled in the car.

Nava stepped into the road. "Hey, doughs!"

The driver braked. The squad swarmed onto the road,

babbling their joy. A ride! Rescue! They were all reaching for the door handles.

"Where you from?" Nava asked the soldiers. They were clearly Force Snafu—green Headquarters company soldiers.

"Honsfeld," said the driver. "We were in an antiaircraft company on the Lanzerath road. Just made it out. How about you chaps?"

Chaps! Ivy League man? Andy wondered.

"Stole a ride on a Jerry tank. You got guests, good buddies. Have to crowd you a little till we can catch another ride."

The driver scowled at the squad. "Jeez, I got springs to think about! I can't afford a breakdown. Got to pick a spot for the gun, chaps. It's right behind us."

Nava took it blankly. The others began to jeer and abuse the clean soldiers in the car. "Chaps, your—" Miles sneered. Embarrassed but adamant, the driver shook his head.

"Sergeant, I'm sorry—"

"You're sorry," Nava sneered. "What happens when the Krauts come along?"

"You'll get a ride. There's other cars behind us."

"I don't hear them."

"They're coming. Well—breaks of the game. I got orders—"

Andy saw Nava move his submachine gun, then scrutinize the men in the back seat. Again he stared at the driver. He spoke quietly.

"By God, I *do* know how it is, soldier, and I'll make a report. You're with that J Company outfit, eh?"

"Yes. I'm sorry, but we gotta go."

"You guys sorry, too?" the sergeant asked the other men.

No one replied. The men gazed in rigid embarrassment down the road. The engine revved up; the car stirred.

"So long, J Company," Nava called. Abruptly he swung his submachine gun. "*Hände hoch!*" he yelled.

Five pink faces stared from under netted helmets. The driver hit the gas, and the car gave a leap like a startled cow. Andy gasped as Nava hosed the soldiers with a stream of ear-splitting shots. They screamed and writhed, their arms flying up. The quiet air shuddered, violated by the terrible noise and the cries of the soldiers. Andy stood there, sick and disbelieving.

Nava's helmet shook as the gun kept chattering. The car tried to climb the bank. Men toppled out like sacks of potatoes. The driver sprawled on the road with a machine pistol in his hand. He fired a brief burst as the squad dived for the ground. Nava drove a stream of slugs into the man. Brokenly, he folded onto his back.

It was silent.

Pop was the first man to sit up. With his helmet askew over one eye, he stared in astonishment at Nava, standing by the car.

"Man, you really *were* tired of walking!"

Andy could not move; he was stunned. Murder: What else was it?

Nava began dragging bodies from the car with one hand. "Come on, idiots—gimme a hand."

"What was that *Hände hoch?*" Andy asked feebly. "Maybe they didn't understand German."

"Like hell. They *are* Germans! Shanks, back the car down."

Shanks let the car coast back onto the road. In silence they searched the bodies. Andy shuddered as he groped for a man's dog tags and found his chest still warm and soft, like the body of a dead rabbit. They found GI documents on the men: payroll records, dog tags, letters. The letters were old and there were no recent entries on their payroll records. All their weapons were German—Schmeisser machine pistols, potato-masher grenades under their coats.

As they wiped blood from the seats, the sergeant snorted:

" 'Chaps'! Clean clothes. And they bought that 'J Company' garbage."

"There ain't no such thing as J Company, is there?" Shanks said.

"Not in this Army. I just wanted to see if he knew we jump from I to K."

The Mouth took the wheel, and the sergeant sat beside him reading a map. Shanks twisted the switch and the starter turned and turned with a raw grinding, as though it were pulverizing coffee. Andy held his breath. The engine barked to life, and the big car, like a willing old horse, groaned over the summit and down the grade into a long valley.

Eyes streaming with the freezing wind, they sat grinning like fools. Wheels beneath them! Man's greatest invention— the body in motion while the feet were at rest! Andy savored the sensation, like a tramp sniffing odors from a kitchen.

After a half hour of lurching along frozen ruts, across ridges, down another valley bordered by tiny farms, they came to a crossroads. Shanks parked in the middle of it and the silence rose about them. There was no sign of life. By the road stood a reeling fingerpost. The top bar pointed west.

Moderscheid—Malmédy

The lower bar pointed south.

Meyerode—St. Vith

"South, baby!" Leo urged. "Let's roll!" He smacked the side of the car with his wet woolen glove.

Shanks started to feed the car a little gas, but Nava barked, "Knock that off."

Standing up, he gazed across the hills to the south. In silence they followed his glance. Columns of smoke leaned on the wind. An observation plane rocked on the air currents.

"South, hell," he snorted. "They're already fighting down there. That's a combat zone, now, Lions. You looking for thrills?"

Andy's eyes misted with chagrin. Via Malmédy, it was at least a two-hour drive to St. Vith; they could be there in fifteen minutes by taking the south road.

He sighed. How's things in Ward 82A, Brother Tom? Are you still swapping comics with your buddies? The boredom must be terrible. Is the wreck in the red bathrobe still looking for an acey-deucy-dicey game? You poor slob! Locked up in that warm hospital. How long since I visited you last? A week?

Only a week?

While Shanks turned the big car west, Andy wiped his glasses on his damp handkerchief. In gloom and apprehension, he gazed out at another dismal forest. . . .

They came soon to Moderscheid, an alcove in the woods filled with stained plaster houses and a bombed-out café. Belgians peered through the curtains at them as they passed. There were no GI's in sight, and they drove on through.

A narrow bridge over a muddy little river—the Amblève—stopped them a few miles farther.

Nava dismounted and stood on the bridge, contemplating the stream. He kicked a chunk of frozen mud in the water.

"It ain't much," he said, "but it'd stop a tank. Why ain't there somebody here to blow it?"

He craned over the side to look for explosives taped to the supports. Shaking his head, he returned to the car.

"If we had any TNT, I'd blow it myself. Of course, there *could* be a division of our own stuff coming this way to stop that column, and they'd need it. In a well-run war, a man would know those things. According to the map, there's another bridge three miles past the next crossroads. They're probably setting a roadblock there right now. . . ."

"Probably," Pop said cynically. "Oh, no doubt."

A drizzle fell, soaking them and turning the road into a brown gelatin smeared over iron. The next town was Ligneuville, a crooked village in a dense forest, its main street almost too narrow for tank traffic. A tent-town pattern of squares on the earth showed where a detachment had been camped outside the town until recently. Silent villagers watched them move around.

"They musta had word the redcoats were coming," Leo said.

At the far end of the village, Andy made out a fingerpost with a collection of boards nailed to it. One of the boards clearly pointed south. He touched Nava's arm excitedly.

"Look, Sarge! There's a crossroads down there—"

"I got eyes," Nava said. "The road goes to St. Vith, too, but *we* aren't going to St. Vith until we get a bridge blown. That armored column could be snapping at our tails right now. Don't forget, we wasted a good hour hiking before we got this car."

He glanced back, then muttered an order, and they piled into the car.

Again they were slithering along the muddy road. The windshield wiper scraped back and forth with a monotony and feebleness that made Andy think of an overtaxed heart. Vito kept peering back to see if they were being followed.

Nava, compulsive map reader, studied the soggy sheet of paper on his lap, as Andy stole worried glances at it too.

"We'll cross that little river again pretty soon," muttered Nava. "And then again just this side of a town called Stavelot. That river must have learned geography from a snake. Five-six miles. There's *got* to be Combat Engineers around *somewheres.*"

"There she is!" Shanks reported, as they limped around a turn.

There she was. Another small stone bridge built by peasants for wagons, but just the breadth of a Tiger tank. With barely enough fall to make a current, the Amblève flowed from south to north, cutting the road cleanly. It was a small stream, but its banks were steep: a perfect tank trap.

Nava clumped onto the bridge and began looking it over as critically as though he were thinking of buying it. Andy followed, shivering. Everyone but Pop got out and joined the sergeant.

"Built like a plowhorse," Nava muttered. "Without dynamite, it'll last a thousand years."

Andy listened to the river *blooping* around the square legs of the bridge, muttering through frozen willow tangles with a sound like old men talking. The wind blew ripples across the water. When he moved, he felt ice crystals in his overcoat collar sawing at his neck.

With a trench knife, Nava dug through frozen slush to the concrete surface of the bridge. Suddenly he straightened. In his face burned a light like sunrise.

"Shanks! Look under the seats of the car!"

"What for?"

"Dynamite! Would anybody send out a team of saboteurs without dynamite?"

Shanks ran to the car. A moment later he yelled: "Mines! TNT! Come and get it or I'll throw it away!"

Nava sent Andy and Apache up the road a short distance to lay mines. They chopped with entrenching tools and bayonets at the taffy-like mud. Beyond them, at a turn, Worden watched for oncoming traffic. The car was parked across the bridge in the trees. The rest of the squad helped Nava to wire the bridge for demolition.

Andy had just lowered a mine into a hole when the sergeant shouted, "Croft! Come here!"

At a plodding trot, the mud turning his shoes to hooves, he hurried to the bridge. Nava held out a detonator box.

"Read this! Which is the positive terminal?"

Andy squinted at the instructions, printed in German. There were technical words he could not translate. But finally, with some knowledge of electricity, he handed it back.

"I can't read it, but I don't think it would make any difference."

"By damn, it better be right."

Andy watched him screw the caps down on the wires. Nava stood up. "Miles, carry the wire for me." He started backing from the bridge to where the car was parked in the woods. Leo trailed after him, paying out wire from a coil. "You'll stay here in the trees with the detonator, Miles. If I fire a shot, turn the key. But don't turn it till I tell you. Croft, get back and finish laying that mine."

They finished wiring the bridge, and under Nava's directions were taping TNT to trees beside the road when Worden came in view, waving his rifle and shouting.

"Armored car on the road!"

Andy was instantly dizzy with the drunkenness of fear. He heard a clatter of track plates, an engine chugging harshly.

Nava bawled, "Kraut car?—For sure?"

Worden ran up, gasping. "I—I think so—"

Andy turned toward the bridge. It was a hundred yards away. The chugging, clanking monster packed with storm troopers—or GI's—was almost upon them. Nava plunged into the trees, the men following him. Andy slapped a wet mitten up to hold his glasses as they slid down his nose. They ran north, then turned left toward the river. Nava halted on the bank and fired the signal shot for Leo.

"Blow her!" he bawled.

Andy stared upstream at the bridge, squinting as he awaited the flash. Nothing happened. He heard the half-track slowing on the road. Nava swore and raised both arms as though already armpit-deep in the water. Like a sleepwalker he stepped from the bank. The brush broke his fall. He floundered out into the stream, waist-deep.

Andy hesitated. But as the others began sliding down the bank, he followed. The cold water seized him like an assassin. He gasped, struggled for breath, finally gathered the strength to wade toward the far bank. Nava was already halfway across, still bawling at Leo to blow the charges.

There was no flash, no roar, nothing but a wail of distress from somewhere in the woods. Nava clambered up the bank, black with wet from the waist down. Andy crawled after him, water gushing from his pants, his boots. Nava and two other men helped Pop out of the river. His face was purple with cold and exertion. Nava led the squad into the woods.

They found Leo kneeling, the detonator between his knees, pounding it against the frozen ground. "Don't work, Sarge!"

Nava gave the brass key a spin, and cursed. "Get in the car! They musta seen the mines or we'd've heard an explosion. Those great German engineers! Lotta bunk. Can't even build a decent detonator—"

Andy sank down in the back seat as the big car lurched onto the road. He heard shouts from beyond the bridge. Nava swung the wheel and tramped on the gas pedal. Andy looked back. Field-gray soldiers stood peering over the shield of an armored car. Its machine gun began to spit flame. Rushing, birdlike objects passed above Andy's head; then the clatter of the gun jangled the air.

There was a *pop!* Nava swore and wrestled the wheel. The car's left rear dropped; the front wheels headed for the ditch. Andy heard the *chunk! chunk! chunk!* of other machine-gun bullets digging into the body of the car.

A flash lit the trees beside the road. Everyone yelled and ducked. Thinking it was a shellburst, Andy waited for fragments to mangle the car. But when the roar came, it was from far behind them. Apache looked back. "They're burning! They hit a mine!"

Andy's glasses had fallen off, giving him a somewhat soapy view of a twisted half-track athwart the road. Angry red flames played about it. Injured men were crawling on the road, and rags of clothing hung from the branches of trees.

The hulking, mud-daubed car wallowed west under the dismal cloud cover. Cold and anxiety tightened on Andy. He felt his wet clothes freezing. This miserable war! This fear that burned in you like a disease! The road deteriorated, the blown tire flopped beneath the fender. Nava would not change it, saying that it gave better traction than the other driving wheel. It was about four miles to the next crossing of the Amblève, he said, at the town of Stavelot.

"I done *everything* to that detonator," Leo whined.

"Can't win 'em all," Nava said. "By hell, we slowed 'em down."

"For how long?" Andy asked.

"Anybody's guess. The main column would be a mile or two behind the scout cars."

"What's this next burg?" Shanks asked. "Big Army town?"

"It's a map center and fuel dump. Ought to mean a lot of tough MP's around, but with our luck all there'll be is librarians and service-station attendants."

He fed the car more gas. The road narrowed, grew muddier, more twisting. Could tanks negotiate it? Andy wondered, with hope. But if they couldn't have, the Germans wouldn't be on it, he decided, having fought back and forth over this country since about A.D. 1200. The wind stung his neck; the shadowless cold thickened toward dusk.

"Stamp your feet," Nava said suddenly. "Get that circulation going. By the numbers—! *Hup, hoop, heep, hope!* Lemme hear you count cadence, Lions! *Hup, hoop—*"

They stamped and counted cadence. Water squished inside Andy's boots. Beside him, Pop croaked out the cadence, his eyes watering in the arctic wind. Andy looked at the others with a sudden feeling of ridiculousness. His last hold on military dignity weakened. He grinned. They looked like a basketball team stormbound on the way to Eagle Rock to play for the championship. Their bus driver was trying to keep them from freezing to death.

Nava glanced at the squad, and Andy saw him grin, too. "Lions," he said "you remind me of my favorite hymn:

> *"I am Jesus' little man,*
> *Yes, by Jesus Christ I am!"*

Shanks gave a nervous giggle, then laughed. Worden laughed, too. Andy felt a yelp of hysteria scratching inside his chest, then unexpectedly roared out a laugh. They were all laughing, sitting there in the dusk shaking with cold and hysteria. Then Nava started braying *Rodger Young!*

> *"To the everlasting glory of the infantry—!*
> *Shines the name,*
> *Shines the name—"*

"—Of Rodger Young!" bawled the Lions.

It was suddenly quiet, everyone breathless. Pop said, "Don't you just love the Army? The sings, and all?"

Without warning, the woods opened up. The laughter broke. The left rear wheel's *thunka-thunka-thunka* slowed as they ran out on a wooded bluff. Where the road turned down the bluff, Nava parked.

Below them lay a wide river valley brimming with dusk. On its north bank lay a village of drab buildings clustered about a small marketplace. Farms and woods divided up the level ground beside the river. Andy heard a deep, surflike roar. Wind? Armor?

Nava pointed up the valley. "Look yonder—all the trucks in Belgium, by God! They must be moving the fuel dump."

The trucks were climbing the bluffs across the valley and turning into the hills. It was too dark to see where they came from. But Andy saw a paved road coming down the valley, touching the marketplace, and making a right-angle turn there to follow the river as it flowed west down the Amblève River. There were two-story structures around the marketplace, and trees, fences, and smaller buildings between the square and the river. Near the bridge were three brick buildings resembling old-time orphanages.

"Stavelot, you miserable mudhole," Nava said, shifting gears, "if it was up to me, I'd hand you over. You don't look worth defending."

He started down the steep, muddy road. Pop leaned forward and tapped his shoulder.

"I don't suppose," he said, "you could drop me off somewhere in that town? There must be a place to go on sick call. I just ain't up to all this, Sergeant."

Nava gave his frowning attention to the road. "I'll do what I can, Pop. Depends on what the situation is down there. I figure the bridge should be well defended, and they won't need us. But didn't you tell me you were a machine gunner in World War I?"

Pop's eyes blinked and watered in the wind. "Yes, but that was a long time ago. *Long* time ago . . ." He blew his nose. He chuckled.

"First night in the trenches, this little French officer leads me and my buddy to our machine-gun nest. He points all around. *'Boches ici! Boches ici!'* Boches everywhere! And in the morning, that's where they came from—everywhere. We stacked them up like cordwood, too."

Leo leered at him. "Did you get the Mailman's Medal?"

"Now that you mention it," Pop said, "I did get cited once or twice."

"So actually," the sergeant said, thoughtfully, "you've had more experience than these kids of mine, huh?"

Pop gazed across the valley at the unbroken line of trucks jostling off into the hills. His mouth turned down glumly. "Well, I—you could say so, I guess. Although—"

"And if they've got any machine guns at the bridge, they may need machine gunners, right?"

"I ain't going into combat with no unfamiliar weapons," Pop grumbled.

"Same identical gun they used twenty years ago."

Pop scrubbed his whiskery chin. "Feed the belt in—work the bolt twice—same old deal?"

"Same old deal," Nava said.

Pop sank deeper into his bundle of clothing. "Wish to God I'd never enlisted. But, okay. I'll stay till tomorrow if I'm needed."

Andy patted the old man's knee. Probably Pop didn't know, himself, why he was staying. Something like the old bull of the herd hating to back out of a fight before the young ones. What Pop knew was that he was about as likely to see tomorrow as he was to grow hair again. Yet he was staying. If I was Pop, Andy thought, I'd be climbing out of this car right now.

The cold of the river valley swallowed them remorselessly as they descended. Night tightened itself on the country. The town across the river seemed to have been laid out without plan, a line of ugly plaster buildings here, a stone shed there, trees, outhouses, sheds scattered about. But the bridge, as they neared it, looked solid, practically immortal.

Two overcoated GI's with tommy guns jumped from behind a wall to flag them down. The car slid around like a boat as Nava stopped it.

"Hands ontoppa your heads!" one of the soldiers said.

"Wh-wh-who won the Series this year?" the other soldier stammered.

"Hell, soldier, I'm a football fan, myself." Nava laughed. "But Roy Rogers is the King of the Cowboys, and Dale Evans is the Queen of the West. That answer your question?"

The guards frowned at each other. There seemed some question about the patriotism of a man who did not follow the World Series.

"Okay," the second man stammered.

"What's your outfit?" Nava asked.

"Two-nine-one Combat Engineers. We're layin' mines and setting charges on the bridge. There's just one squad of us, though."

"You mean to say that with all those trucks," Nava demanded, "there's only one squad to defend this bridge?"

"That's all. Everybody else is moving maps and gasoline. We don't even have wire yet."

One of the Engineers led the car past some men chopping holes in the road. Mines were stacked in a ditch. At the far end of the little bridge, Andy saw one of the tall, grim buildings he had noticed from above—three stories of dark brick and tiny windows. A technical sergeant hurried from the building as they parked.

"Am I ever glad to see you guys!" he blurted. "You with that armored infantry company?"

"Just casuals, Sergeant. We're about two jumps ahead of a German armored column."

"Oh, Lord!" the sergeant said. "We ain't even got wire yet! We just got here a half hour ago."

"How come you don't have a road guard at the top of the bluff?" Nava asked. "They could be up there right now, drawing a bead on us."

"Couldn't spare a man! And hell, all we ever done before is build Bailey bridges. Look, I'm Sergeant Yates. If you got any ideas—"

"Abe Nava, Sergeant. I got an idea your men had better scratch up some wire if they have to chop down telephone poles to get it. And we'd better manage a road guard, between us. I guess I'll take over, since I rank you," he added.

Yates drew a breath. "Fine. It's all yours."

Nava sent Apache in Yates's jeep up to the top of the bluffs. He dispatched two men to get wire, and picked teams to man the Engineers' few weapons. Then he sent Pop and

Vito into one of the buildings with a light machine gun, two of Yates's men into another. Everyone was stumbling around looking for things and asking questions.

"Croft, Miles—" Nava said. "Take one of the bazookas behind that wall. Miles, have you fired it?" Leo bobbed his head. "Okay. Croft will load," Nava said.

". . . Pretty sure they're coming?" Andy heard Yates ask Nava, as he grubbed for rockets in a truck.

"Nothin's for sure, Yates. The half-track we stopped mighta been just reconnoitering. If I was a tank commander, I'd turn north at that last little burg, Ligneuville. From there it's just a jump to Malmédy and a paved road. This lower road is barely passable."

"That's right," Yates said quickly, eager to believe. "That's the Malmédy highway up at the other end of town, where them trucks are. Be a lot faster for them, right?"

"Except that Malmédy's more liable to be defended," Nava said. "So I don't know.—By the way, who's 'them'?"

"All I know is what the major said when he sent us down from Malmédy. A German armored regiment knocked over the Büllingen gas dump this morning. They refueled and pulled out again. There's an armored infantry company coming to lend a hand here. My orders are to hold at all costs till they get here."

Andy carried an armload of rockets behind the high stone wall Nava had pointed out. Punctured with slot-like openings, it looked like a fragment of a building that had been carried away by a cyclone. One end was anchored to the building next door. Leo pawed away some rubble beneath a window opening and propped the bazooka against the wall.

"Jeez, I'm freezing!" he said.

Andy felt his pants and shoes congealing. His feet were so numb that when he walked he stumbled. Suddenly he remembered that his pack, at least, had not got wet when they waded across the river. He found the dry socks Nava had scrounged for them in Honsfeld. They both changed, then made a couple of tiny caverns in the rubble and started some heat tablets burning. They steamed their shoes and mittens and rubbed their feet.

Andy got up and glanced through the window. The dark Ardennes wind, whetted on snow and ice, brought tears to his eyes and drove him back to the little nucleus of heat. The tablets burned with a faint bluish glow.

Just as they were pulling on their steaming, spongy shoes, a rifle popped on the bluffs. Echoes cascaded down the valley. Apache's jeep was howling down the road.

"Posts!" Nava bawled in the darkness.

The sergeants waited near the wall as Apache drove over the bridge. The jeep stopped, and Apache gasped out a report: A whole column of tanks led by a couple of armored cars was on the road!

Yates immediately wanted to blow the bridge. It was wired, tested, and ready to go.

"Slow down," Nava said. "If our reinforcements come soon enough, the brass will want to put some antitank guns across the river."

New sounds rose above the muted road of trucks still hauling gasoline into the hills. Deep engines burbled and track plates clashed.

Nava swept the cliffs with binoculars. "They're stopping —probably leery of our trucks."

Nava and Yates moved off.

A few minutes later some tanks started down the grade. Shanks came running to the wall where Andy and Leo peered anxiously through the window.

"You guys ready?"

With a rocket in his hands, Andy nodded. "What's the word?"

"Three tanks coming, probably reconnoitering. If the mines don't stop them, the Engineers will blow the bridge."

"I've got to see those Engineers blow anything but their noses," Andy said gloomily.

The noise swelled as the tanks rounded a hill at the base of the bluff. A rifle popped; a parachute flare whistled aloft, and a pattern of chalky light swung back and forth over the road. Suddenly the tanks rolled into the light, led by a Panther showing a German flag on its antenna. The Panther halted. A searchlight on its deck suddenly blazed on.

Andy ducked.

Shadows ran and reeled as the white beam scalded river, buildings, and road. The light blinked. There was a flash, followed by the shriek of an incoming shell. Lightning struck the adjacent building with a crash. Bricks thundered down as smoke and dust billowed. From the darkness came yelling, glass chiming down in showers, and Nava's voice bawling:

"Hold your fire! They're trying to find us."

A second shell screamed in. A tinkling rain of glass fell to the street. Andy crouched against the wall; the blinding flash lit the inside of his skull; the blast hurt his eardrums.

The light blinked out. Seconds later he heard the Panther charging the bridge.

All the military will leaked out of him as he fumbled with the flash goggles. All he could think of was *Run! Run!* Why didn't they blow the damned bridge?

He heard Leo babbling, "This thing is jammed on safety!"

Andy tried to help him get the launcher off safety. They cursed each other's clumsiness. As they grappled with it, a flash lit the scene like a giant flashbulb. A shock wave ran under their feet. Startled, they stared across the river. Andy saw the bow of the Panther lift like an assault boat hitting a wave. A ball of golden light engulfed it, then died. The Panther whirled out of control. It had detonated a mine. With a crackling roar and a burst of Roman-candle effects, the ammunition rack in the tank's stern exploded. The escape hatches opened; men in coveralls and black Tam-o'-Shanter caps spilled out on the road.

Nava shouted for fire.

Machine-gun tracers sailed the river like slow, floating fireflies. Leo found the safety at last, and aimed. A rocket hissed away, its short tail burning fiercely. Somewhere in the building at their right, a machine gun began to rattle. A rocket flashed over the bridge from the other bazooka downriver. Andy shoved another round into the bell of the launcher. As he leaned away from the blast, he could see wounded tankers lying on the road in the white cone of the flare.

"I hit the brute! I hit it!" Leo yelled.

Andy looked. A bonfire flickered on the deck of the second tank. But in a moment it failed. Both remaining tanks now wheeled, and in a few seconds they went clanking back up the road.

After a few minutes Nava and Yates ran out to check casualties and order more ammunition up. There were no wounded. Nava brought some rockets and told Andy and Leo to eat some rations and keep their eyes open.

An hour passed. A jeep whined boldly down the street from the marketplace, parked near the bridge, and Andy saw a passenger stand up in it.

"Whoever's in charge report here on the double!" the man shouted.

Nava ran from the basement where he had established his command post. Andy caught snatches of conversation

—enough to learn that a company of armored infantry was arriving right behind the jeep and that the man Nava was talking to was the commanding officer.

"They must have tanks, huh?" Leo said to Andy. "What *is* armored infantry, anyway?"

Andy had no idea; but in a few minutes dozens of anxious riflemen were detrucking by the river, and some dainty little antitank guns—small cannons just too big to fire corks, he thought—were rolled across the river. Judging by the confusion and the treble voices, the reinforcements were almost as young, and certainly as scared, as the Lions. Noncoms put them to work digging emplacements and carrying weapons into the somber brick buildings along the river.

The cold bore down mercilessly. Subfreezing air crisped Andy's nostrils when he breathed. Trembling, he kindled more GI heat in the rubble, and crouched before it. Leo poured water into their cups, and they heated it with powdered coffee. The hot drink restored them a little, but exhaustion and cold had finished them. They began falling asleep in the midst of speaking. Andy ceased to be sure of what he imagined and what was real.

About midnight two shivering riflemen were led up to relieve them. Nava collected his team, and they stumbled to the basement of a building. A switchboard had been set up here. A major, some noncoms, and a few junior officers hurried about. The major was shouting into a telephone:

"Yessir, patrols are out. No report yet, but the men we relieved say it's that large armored column. I'd like to pull my antitank guns back and destroy the bridge— I know that, Colonel, but—"

Nava led the men toward a cell off the basement. Andy heard the major say, in disappointment:

"All right. In any event the mines should give us time to blow the bridge in case of—"

The Lions milled about by candlelight in a damp cell smelling of mice and mildew. Nava made them unroll packs and change to dry long johns and trousers. With all its defects, the cellar seemed to Andy like Grand Hotel after the raw wind outside. They rubbed their feet. He worried about the bridge. Someone, some light colonel twenty miles back who was not looking down the barrel of a cannon, was willing to wait till the last minute to demolish the Stavelot bridge. He crawled into his sleeping bag, heaved a sigh, and fell into a deathlike sleep.

CHAPTER NINE

Near St. Vith, Belgium
17 December

Tom woke to the rolling boom of artillery. Stiff and cold, he reared up, anxiety clutching at his heart. In a corner of a half-demolished barn, a tiny fire wept smoke and driblets of flame. Near it, standing by a broken wall, he saw Corporal Collins and Lieutenant Fox gazing out across a countryside dismal under sagging clouds.

Dully, he remembered arriving last night, too tired to drive farther. Collins had wanted to keep heading west on the Malmédy highway, past the river towns of Malmédy, Stavelot, Trois Ponts. On to Liège—and freedom! But the lieutenant had insisted on turning south to St. Vith.

So here they were, poised between lost and unlost, on the road to St. Vith. Or somewhere.

He looked out at a landscape with the dead gray tones of an underexposed photograph. New snow frosted the road. Southeast, the wind felled tall columns of smoke standing where big shells were exploding along a road.

Tom relaxed. The action was distant. Yet it was plain that the enemy had clawed miles deeper into their front during the night.

"Climb out of there, Croft," the lieutenant said gruffly,

glancing around. He looked grim. His voice was ragged with the misery of a hangover. Squatting by the fire, he resumed heating a meat ration.

Tom felt headachy, with an ominous tingle behind his Adam's apple. Apprehensively, he cleared his throat. A cold in this country was kissing kin to pneumonia.

"Let's go! It's after ten," the lieutenant snapped.

Surprised, Tom frowned as he buckled his leggings. You don't kid me any, Sidney, he thought. Makes a man feel better about himself to have somebody to order around, doesn't it? You Tarzan, me GI Joe. Yet a flicker of shame made him wince as he remembered using Andy for the same purpose —a shadow to prove to himself that he was solid. Andy had not objected too much, needing the arrangement at least as much as Tom, whose support and protection were always there.

If this nut lands us back in combat, he thought, I hope I've got a few guys to give orders to. Somebody to take my mind off myself.

Huddled around the little fire, they devoured lukewarm hash and coffee. Whisker stubble blurred the lieutenant's jaws. He rose. "Finish up and let's get going," he said.

Parked inside the barn, the jeep snorted to life. Tom stowed his gear. Fox drove out to the road and compared the country with a map. Tom joined him, holding a canteen cup of coffee, and tried to relate the map's lines and shadings to the frozen landscape. He saw a town, *Malmédy,* labeled on the main east-west route. Miles below it, straddling a highway that paralleled the Malmédy route, lay St. Vith. Winding roads, some probably impassable, webbed the countryside between the two large towns. They must be on one of these secondary roads, he decided.

Collins wandered out and looked at the sky like a sailor.

Fox saw that he had not brought out his gear. "Damn it, get your stuff, Corp!" he barked.

"You're heading for St. Vith, huh?" Collins asked.

"That's the general idea."

"I'm going to base hospital in Liège—it's on my evacuation tag. I'll hike up to the main road and catch a ride."

Tom looked at him in surprise. The lieutenant turned to stare fully at the corporal.

"Maybe I'd better see that evacuation tag before you start," he said.

Collins's puffy eyes returned his gaze. He grinned. "Maybe we better see what's in that crate we risked our necks to get for you."

"Booze," the lieutenant said. "What about it?"

"Army Regulations cover the rescue of booze under fire?"

Fox leaned back. He pulled up his lower lip.

"I'm sorry you didn't understand why I drafted you. I had to destroy some papers and bury my men. In this country foxes eat corpses, and I was still responsible for them, dead or alive. Also, I wanted to make sure the patrol I'd sent out hadn't come back. I had no permission to pull out. I could get court-martialed for it. As long as I was there, I decided to rescue my booze. You see?"

Collins's brow creased. What he saw was that he was out-lawyered.

"I'm taking you along," the lieutenant added, "because you may be needed. A divisional town ought to be able to take care of itself, but St. Vith was long on cooks and musicians, and short on riflemen when I left. Put your gear in the car."

Collins scraped the whiskers on his jaws, grunted, and heaved his barracks bag into the jeep.

They started south down the miserable farm road. Ten minutes later, the jeep struggled up to a windy ridge, and they heard, with shock, a prolonged roar of engines below them. It sounded to Tom as if a hive of giant bees had been disturbed. The lieutenant swore sharply and swerved the car into a thicket.

Stunned, they stared upon a column of German tanks and trucks coiling across hills and farms to the east, and crawling from view into a forest to the west. Miles long, the column's head and tail were out of sight.

"My God!" Fox said. "That must be the outfit that knocked us out of the Losheim Gap yesterday!"

Collins moaned. "Don't nobody but 2nd Division know how to blow a bridge? Nobody's laid a hand on them Krauts."

Fox, swearing under his breath, began calculating. "There's a big gas dump at Malmédy. That's probably where the Krauts will have lunch. The spearhead may be there already. We'll have to sit here till the last tank passes."

"Ain't there a road to Spa this side of Malmédy?" Collins suggested. "Maybe if—"

Fox shook his head. They settled down to the only action they could take: silent prayer.

Tanks gave way to trucks; to armored cars stuffed with infantry; to service and supply vehicles. Finally there remained only an odd straggler or two, hurrying to catch up.

The crossroads was deserted. The lieutenant started the car. They rushed down the hill, bumped across the mauled and muddy road, and sped south.

Somewhere in his faulty but inventive brain, the lieutenant seemed to have all the roads of the Ardennes Plateau tattooed. They stole through frozen farmlands and snowy forests, then up a final rise from the top of which they gazed south at a town on a low hill.

"St. Vith, we have come," Fox said cheerfully.

Collins muttered something. Tom gazed down at the town, caught in a web of six converging roads. Light traffic flicked along the paved east-west road. Other roads tangled in a knot at the heart of the town, which clutched the hilltop like a stone starfish. A railroad touched the town's eastern edge.

Uneasily, Tom felt the war's presence. Artillery thundered behind storm clouds. Observation planes snored in the sky.

They crossed the highway and drove up a steep road into St. Vith. The town had an arctic look—gray buildings, gray sky, bare trees. Tom guessed it might have, at the most, one frost-free month in the year. The soldiers they saw darted uneasy glances at them; one man ducked into an alley.

"As it says in my history of the 422nd Regiment," the lieutenant observed, "morale was unusually high in St. Vith in December—early December, that is."

He drove up to a cluster of stone buildings at the heart of the town. Two trucks with steaming exhausts idled before a building with a peaked roof and a small forest of chimneys. He parked near one of the trucks. A collection of bewildered soldiers huddled on the road. A helmeted master sergeant with a cigar in his mouth stepped out of the headquarters building and shouted for attention.

"Any you goldbricks ain't had infantry basic?" he bawled.

Nearly all the men raised their arms.

"You men that ain't had basic line up over here. You're riflemen," he said.

The men began to call out startled protests.

"Move, damn it!" the sergeant barked. "You—staff sergeant, there—take over and form 'em into ranks. Rest of you

men line up behind the other truck—you're going out as automatic-weapons teams and mortarmen—"

The men argued as they were shouted into ranks. Again the door opened, and Tom saw a big, natty lieutenant step out, shuddering as the wind struck him. He stepped into the shelter between the jeep and a truck. His face, smooth, pink, and unlined, looked like a retouched photograph. In his hand he held a fluttering sheet of onionskin paper.

"Well, look who's here!" said Lieutenant Fox, with surprise and pleasure. "Fred Sparks—old Sparky himself. Had the desk next to me."

Lieutenant Sparks called indignantly to the sergeant. "Good Lord, Sergeant! I thought the men had left by now. Colonel Nungesser just called again from the roadblock, asking where his reinforcements were."

The heavyset top sergeant about-faced niftily. "Been dragging men out of hiding places all over town, Lieutenant. They'll be going right out."

"How many have had combat experience?"

"Well, uh—none that I know of, sir."

The lieutenant winced. Tom closed his eyes. They're looking right at us! he thought, in panic. "Well, get them moving," Sparks said. "And any other reinforcements you can scrape up."

"What about that combat command from 7th Armored, sir? Can I tell the men it's on the way?"

"Left Aachen on schedule. All we know."

Lieutenant Fox climbed out and charged up to him as he turned to reenter the building. "Hey, Sparky!" He offered his hand, grinning.

Sparks gave him a blank stare, then met his handclasp nervously. "Judas Priest, Sid! Thought you'd had it. What are you doing back here?"

"Regrouping. Isn't everybody?"

Lieutenant Sparks lowered his voice after a quick glance at the headquarters building. "Did you have written authority to pull back?"

"Pull back?" Fox laughed, and looked at Tom. "Hell, we just ran, like everybody else that wasn't dead. They were firing *shells* at us, Sparky, not erasers. It's a real war out there. I didn't have written permission, but I had a lot of encouragement from the Jerries."

Friendship and firmness tussled in Sparks's face. "You'd better be thinking about what you're going to say, Sid. According to one report we've had, your whole group pulled out yesterday and left the Losheim Gap wide open. Now we've got Krauts coming out of our ears!"

"My outfit did all this?" Fox asked.

"It's probably a combination of foulups," Lieutenant Sparks hedged, "but—"

Tom realized suddenly that here, at Divisional Headquarters, they knew less about what was happening than he did. All this talk about fixing blame—! When the whole sector was boiled like a disturbed anthill.

"What's the damage so far?" Fox asked.

"Complete snafu. Communications are so shot we don't really know the extent of our losses. A panzer force came within four miles of here an hour ago and ducked back." His voice broke a little. "There may not even *be* a 106th Division by the time all the reports are in!"

Tom's belly muscles knotted. With a fluttering in his ears, he saw ghost figures in a deathly place like the Monschau Forest—ghosts with faces like Andy, Rotunno, Shanks.

Were they all dead now?

The trucks were loading, anxious faces peering from the dark canvas caverns.

"Where's the roadblock?" asked Lieutenant Fox.

Sparks pointed. "Other side of that ridge—straddling the Schönberg highway."

Below the town, the highway trailed east a mile and plunged out of sight in a wooded ridge flowing like a reef over the snowy plateau. Low and black, it resembled an inkblot upon the frozen landscape. Beyond the ridge, the road mysteriously reappeared to run east into the storm clouds that hid the Schnee Eifel and the enemy.

"You'd better follow the trucks down," Lieutenant Sparks said. "If I were you, I'd report to Colonel Nungesser, at the roadblock. Make yourself useful—get a medal or something. When all the reports are in, the pullout may blow over."

The lieutenant nodded gravely. "I'll do that—buzz on down and get my head shot off. Why don't you get inside, Sparky? You're shivering."

"Play it any way you want, Sid, but—"

"Where's a dispensary? The corporal has a touch of trench foot."

"All the medics are setting up aid stations at the roadblock. Help yourself to socks and foot powder at the supply room. I'll cover for you if your name comes up."

"Cover for me!" Fox chuckled as the door closed. "Sparky, you couldn't cover a postage stamp with an Indian blanket."

The Schönberg highway was now bare of traffic except for the jeep bustling importantly toward the ridge. At the wheel, humming to himself, sat Lieutenant Fox, locked once more in the Bluebeard's chamber of his private thoughts. Pulling on new socks and overshoes, Tom examined his own anxieties tenderly. He had a feeling of hollowness, of fear putting out poisonous shoots like a vine.

The car entered the lee of the ridge, and the cold seemed

to squeeze the very light out of the air. A moment later they were swallowed by a dark woods filled with the somber organ tones of the wind in the pines. It was a cold and terrifying place—a sniper's dream. The tree trunks were as slender as saplings, but soared forty or fifty feet, packed so closely that their branches meshed into a tangle. The bottom of a well got more sunlight than this miserable forest, he thought.

The lieutenant spoke.

"I'm going to volunteer you men for squad leaders—platoon if necessary."

Tom started. Collins snorted. "You kidding? Croft's had only one day in combat, and I'm strictly a BAR man."

"That's *our* secret. Somebody who's been in combat will have to keep those career cooks and mechanics from panicking when the stuff starts flying. Today's live Pfc. may be tomorrow's tech. sergeant."

Collins shrugged. He did not seem to care one way or the other. But Tom, recalling with a flash of shame that he had told himself all he needed was someone to lead, vigorously shook his head.

"Not me!"

"Don't sell yourself short. There is something I call creative cowardice. A man gets so scared he does things he wouldn't believe himself capable of."

"I had a buddy like that on D day," Collins recalled. "He got so scared he shot himself in the foot. That what you mean?"

Fox sighed. "Not exactly, Corp."

The road crossed a summit, and coasted. Soon an aperture could be seen in the trees. They began to pass military vehicles and soldiers stringing wire and carrying supplies. A GI sprang into the road holding a rifle at long thrust, as though to bayonet the jeep in the radiator. The lieutenant braked sharply.

"Name, rank, and s-s-serial—!" the guard stammered.

Fox identified himself. "Which way to Battalion, soldier?"

"Hundred and fifty yards down that telephone line, sir."

The lieutenant parked and strode off into the forest. Tom was numb with the suddenness of the return to combat. He watched men taping clusters of TNT blocks, the size and shape of cigarette packs, to the red-barked pine trees. Others were digging emplacements or unloading trucks.

"Platoon sergeant," Collins snorted, looking at Tom. "I can see you now, new boy."

Tom slowly shook his head in agreement. In the east, storm clouds sagged upon the horizon. The highway, after leaving the trees, ran down a long slope with a line of leafless poplars at the left. Several hundred yards along, two trucks were parked, probably the ones from St. Vith. Men were jumping from them.

The lieutenant returned and drove on.

"Where we going?" Collins asked suspiciously.

"They need men down where those trucks are," Fox said, looking chilled and grim.

Staring down the road, Tom shivered.

"They don't need *us,* damn it!" Collins said.

"They need us. The few men that know what they're doing will be kept here at the main line of resistance. There's one good man, Sergeant Howell, at the outpost. Old Army and plenty of experience. We'll help his group lay mines and set a roadblock. There'll only be about twenty of us until that combat command arrives. I told the colonel you could each take a squad, if the sergeant wants you to. It may grow into a platoon pretty fast."

Collins said something profane, and shook his head.

Tom began to argue. "Sir, I—what if—"

"All you'll have to do is to tell the men to keep their tails down. And keep them firing. The sergeant will set up the defense."

Near the end of the line of poplars, Tom saw men prying up chunks of pavement to lay antitank mines. In bleak fields bordering the road, other soldiers were digging in the earth like peasants, throwing up black rings of soil on the snow around their entrenchments. A tall man in a field jacket, wearing a first sergeant's chevrons, was handing out entrenching tools to shivering GI's. They took them and ran out to start digging. In sudden anger, the sergeant shouted at a pair of soldiers digging in the field on the south.

"No, you morons! Ah said twenty yards from the road, not fifty."

The lieutenant parked, and led the men up to the sergeant. Tom guessed this was Howell, the sergeant Fox had mentioned. He was saying to some men huddled nervously nearby:

"Lug some bazooka rounds out to where them two men are digging." Then he saw the lieutenant. "Yessir?"

Fox introduced himself. "I'll be your platoon leader, Sergeant."

The sergeant had a dark, thin, hawkish face, with opalescent eyes of the glacial blue of skimmed milk. In his stubbled cheeks were pockets like thumbholes in biscuit dough.

"It ain't exactly a platoon so far," he said. "Only twenty-odd goldbricks you couldn't rightly call soldiers."

The lieutenant smiled. "Fine. I'm only a twenty-man platoon leader myself. The colonel sent me down here to study with an expert."

The sergeant shrugged, and Tom felt his keen, appraising stare. "These men with you?"

"Yes. The corporal has been in the line since D day. Croft's been with 2nd Division recently. Do you want them to take a squad each?"

"They can try. They'll need leg irons to keep them jokers in place when the stuff begins to fly."

"What's the situation?"

"We got bazookas but no bazookamen, machine guns but no gunners. There's an observation post on that next ridge down the road, but no wire laid to it. The observer's got a radio and so has Battalion. The catch is, we ain't."

"We have now," Fox told him. "There's a radio in the jeep."

Tom winced as Howell slapped a gloved hand down on his and Collins's shoulders and squeezed without mercy, as though he could tell, by the quality of a man's groans, something about his leadership ability.

"Git on them fools, now," he said, "before they all buddy up in one big pit. Make sure the ammo's where it's supposed to be. I'll check on you later. Tell your men you'll shoot them if they try to run away. And mean it."

"Off the record"—Lieutenant Fox sounded almost casual —"do you think the Jerries will attack before dark?"

"Anybody's guess. Some tanks bluffed their way up to the OP an hour ago. We got regimental cannon fire on the road and run 'em back. But somebody said our guns are being moved now. So I don't know whether we can count on them again or not."

Woodenly, Tom plodded into the field he was to command. He saw the men watching him, expectantly. The nearest pair, only twenty yards away, stood in a half-finished slit trench, their expressions revealing a hunger for a transfusion of his own supposed courage. In their eyes he probably appeared

the pick of an officer and a first sergeant, one of those com-
batwise veterans they had heard about.

"Hey, fella!"

One of the men in the slit trench jumped out and hurried
toward him. He wore thick eyeglasses and looked as old as
Tom's father. His buddy followed. Both began talking at
once, pleading and conspiratorial.

". . . never even *fahred* a bazooka before!"

"Been running a sawmill with a CE battalion—!"

"On limited service until—"

"Don't even know how to *aim* the bastard!"

Tom faked it as best he could. "Just point it and squeeze
the rounds off. You'll catch on. Whatever weapon you're using, lay the fire down."

He walked on, beginning to perspire.

His eleven men, he discovered, were like any squad a
clamshell digger might have pulled up, dripping wet, out of
any limited-service outfit. He knew they would leap out of
their trenches and head for the woods when the first tank
came up the road. And what could he do about it? Shoot
them?

The voice of the sergeant rang from the other field.

"Armor on the road! Sergeants report to me!"

Tom moaned.

Howell talked like a give-'em-hell football coach. Dusk was
blowing in. Down the road, Tom saw nothing but bending
trees and scurrying snow devils. He shook uncontrollably.

"Stay on your men," Howell said. "Give 'em hell. If you
don't cuss 'em out, they won't even shoot. When I call for
fire, see to it they lay it down. The signal will be a smoke
grenade. What's amatter, Croft?—Got the GI's?"

Tom gulped and shook his head. "No, I—"

Howell fixed a long-shanked rifle grenade in a rifle. "Take off. The lieutenant and me will be right here."

Tom saw with horror, as he returned, that he had not dug himself a foxhole! He found a half-dug trench and clawed snow over the black clods. In the midst of it, a stomach cramp seized him. When it left, he felt cold and weak.

"Everybody down and stay down!" the bullhorn in Howell's chest roared out. "Tanks are passing the OP. Three Panthers and some personnel carriers. We're gonna blow hell outa them, and don't you forget it—"

In the windy dusk, Tom saw tanks topping the distant rise like matchboxes skidding slowly downwind. Then came the carriers, high and boxy; all dropped from view into a swale, reappearing much closer, with clear outlines and a mastiff growl of engines. He rolled onto his side and desperately hacked at the earth with his helmet to deepen the half-finished trench. *Where's the artillery? Where's the damn' artillery?* He raised his head like a lizard and froze into watchfulness. On they came, and not a shell to slow them. The lousy goldbricking artillery!

Antennae whipping like fly rods, the tanks reached the line of poplars. Close behind came the armored cars.

"Sarge! Sarge!" a man called frantically.

Tom peeked over the lip of the hole. A man named Daniels had raised his head. "Can't find my flash goggles, Sarge!"

"Then close your eyes when you fire. And get your head down!"

Downshifting, snorting, the tanks were abreast and still rolling. The mines! Tom groaned. Hadn't they armed the mines?

The tanks halted. They had seen them! Now they would detour into the field. Like a wounded man entangled in barbed wire, he lay moaning, afraid to move. The cannons would blast them out like ground squirrels. If they ran, machine guns would cut them in two.

The last track plate slapped the road. Engines idled. It was the perfect moment for one of Tom's neurotics to leap from his foxhole and go screaming toward the woods.

There was a rasping noise. He peered across the parapet. A hatch opened on the leading Panther, rising like a hinged saucer to let a man in a billed cap peer out. Coolly, the German stood up, wearing a long, loosely bloused coat and binoculars around his neck. Smoking a cigarette, he scrutinized the woods through the glasses, then spoke to someone in the tank. Numbly, Tom watched him drop to the road.

What went on?

Two other tankers followed. The personnel carriers lumbered into the icy field. Gray-clad foot soldiers, overburdened with equipment, jumped down and took up ten-yard intervals. Kneeling or standing, they lit cigarettes, and waited.

Realization clicked in Tom's head like an electric relay.

The Germans had not seen the mines. They had not noticed the activity in the woods. They were absolutely oblivious of the guns covering them.

The tankers conferred with an infantry officer. Then all glanced at their wristwatches and looked at the sky.

From behind the trees, a grenade lifted in a smoking corkscrew. The rifle report rang sharply an instant later, as the still photograph blurred into a motion picture running wild. German voices shrieked. The infantrymen flopped down or ran for the armored cars. The grenade flowered into a blossom of white smoke on the road.

A few guns popped across the road. A machine gun chattered. Someone bawled his name. "Croft! Get the fire on 'em!"

With a gasp he came to and began screaming at the men around him. "Fire! Fire!"

A few nervous rifles cracked. A machine gun ripped. A rocket laid a streak of incandescence across the field and exploded against a tree. Tom emptied the tommy gun in two bursts, still yelling for fire. Spatters of black iron flecked the white hull of the Panther. The first tanker was hip-deep in the deck hatch when a grenade burst near him. He hung limply overside, as though seasick.

Another man tried to cram him down the hatch, but was knocked down by a rifle shot. A rocket whooshed over from Collins's squad and blasted into the bow of the second tank. Flames seared it, laying on the white road a black pattern of mud.

Tom looked for targets, but the German infantrymen had disappeared into the earth. Their shots snapped past him. He tried to cram a clip into his gun backward, panting in frustration: then he reloaded, and raised his head. The remaining tank was backing off, its siphon-like barrel searching.

The barrel came to rest. Tom was actually looking down it as it fired. Lightning struck the earth near him. The shock nearly broke his back. He flattened himself in the trench. More shells hurtled in. Red-hot fragments hissed in the snow. Then the tank began shelling the other side of the road. Tom tried to call for bazooka fire, but as he lifted his head a bullet blasted dirt into his eyes. He was blind and scared. A machine gun on one of the armored cars began chopping at the field. He heard one of his squad scream.

"Mother! I'm hit!"

It's not happening, Tom thought. A warm numbness wrapped him. It was a nightmare, a terrible dream; he would force himself awake.

"Croft, if you ain't dead, *get them fools firing!*"

Tom looked up, his vision still foggy. He saw the Panther clanking off down the road. Soldiers in long-skirted coats were scrambling aboard the personnel carriers. He cupped his hands and in broken squawks called for fire.

White faces peeked over parapets. Blasted into the snow were smoking shell holes and barrowfuls of black dirt. A weapon at a time, the men began firing, unevenly, like trainees banging away at moving targets. German soldiers dropped, crying out. The firing heated up.

Suddenly the cars made U-turns and clattered back to the road. A rocket detonated behind them. They swayed east into the dusk.

"Cease fire!"

Scattered about in the snow lay two dozen German soldiers. The wounded GI was still screaming. Lieutenant Fox appeared and ran to a tree, the sergeant behind him. They scrutinized the Germans on the road. Then Fox beckoned to Tom. Tom clambered up and stumbled across the field, mumbling to himself.

Night closed in with new fears. As the light failed, Tom imagined hordes of German storm troopers crawling up in the darkness.

The German dead and wounded had been stripped of letters and diaries. The dead were left on the snow, the wounded carried back to the woods. The wounded man in his squad died as an aidman worked over him. He started the other men on a routine of duties like sunset chores on a farm: weapons cleaning, replenishment of ammunition, improvement of entrenchments. The minefield was deepened, and concertinas of barbed wire were strung. At 2100 Fox summoned Tom to the command post across the road.

Collins was there, crouched to hide the spark of his cigarette. A slit trench had been enlarged, and camouflaged with snow and branches. The lieutenant was signing off on the walkie-talkie. Sergeant Howell was profanely trying to get a telephone to work.

"How you doing?" Fox asked Tom.

Tom shrugged.

"Attaboy! You and Corp are taking out a reconnaissance patrol. Pick two of your best men. Leave all written material behind. Corp will show you the ropes, and next time you'll take out your own patrol."

Tom had had little time to evaluate his men, but his first pick was a skinny little man with an East Texas accent. He said they called him Cowboy. He had no upper front teeth, which gave him a slurping diction. Tom's other choice was a man named Rossi, a mechanic from South Dakota, stubby and sleepy-looking, with a thick neck and bloodshot eyes. He was either very steady or very stupid, and it was almost impossible to get more than two words out of him. Tom figured this might be an asset on a patrol.

Collins led them down the dark road toward the observation post. The downslope leveled, and the road began to climb. In twenty minutes they reached the top of another forested ridge. Collins halted the column, deployed it, and clicked out a grenade signal. From the woods at their left, a response cricketed back. A GI emerged from the trees, and he and the corporal conversed.

"Your platoon leader just told me it's confirmed," the observer said. "Setz, up the road, is in German hands. And a place called Wallerode, north of here, has probably folded too."

"The hell with that. All I got to find out is what we're up against here."

"Sight along my rifle. What was left of the force that hit you is bivouacked in the woods there, fifteen hunnert yards away. About 1800 I heard trucks hauling in. Then I heard armor deploying south of the road. When the wind lets up, you can hear infantry, too. And I'll be damned if I ain't even heard horses!"

"Did you take azimuths?"

"You got a nice sense of humor, bud. I couldn't so much as see across the road."

The column trudged on. Tom envied the corporal's sour matter-of-factness. He approached combat like a fry-cook preparing for the rush hour. Collins halted and listened around, then led on another few hundred feet and deployed the men in a ditch.

He removed his helmet, lay beside Tom, and planted a compass between them. Tom was shivering so hard it was physically exhausting. By signs and whispers, Collins decoded for him the enemy's night sounds, then wrote some numbers and symbols on a pad.

In fifteen minutes they were back at the observation post. Collins brought the observer out again.

"Hallelujah!" the man said. "An armored command just hauled in."

Just as they were approaching the roadblock, flashes lit the sky northwest of St. Vith, and there was a long, flying scream of projectiles passing over. The men hit the ground, but Collins merely turned his head to watch the flashes in their rear. A rolling bombardment began to pound the German positions.

They checked in with Howell. The lieutenant was off big-dealing it at Battalion CP, he said.

"If that guy don't get us all killed, he'll make us famous. Right now he's trying to requisition bedsheets for you. It ain't a bad idea—camouflage—like the Krauts whitewashing their tanks for snow fighting. We'll use them on patrols."

"If the sheets come in time," Collins said, "send one to my foxhole, will you? I haven't changed my linen in over a week."

The shelling went on, volley after volley crumpling in the distance. Tom, trying to sleep in the position of a diver doing a two-and-a-half somersault, wondered whether the Germans had not brought up their artillery or were saving ammunition. For some reason they were not hammering back. He was unable, somehow, to regard it as good news.

PART FIVE

The Turning Point

On the night of 17 December, General Sepp Dietrich took time from his troubles at Elsenborn Ridge, where dug-in GI's were slaughtering his Sixth Panzer Army, to berate Colonel Peiper by telephone.

Peiper's blunder in not crossing the Amblève River last night, Dietrich raged, might cost the whole offensive! He had reached the bridge that afternoon—why had he not crossed it to the paved road on the north side? For Peiper had already complained that the dirt road he had been assigned was becoming impassable.

Peiper's answer has never been fully explained. His scouts had reported many vehicles in the vicinity of the bridge at Stavelot; he feared they might be tanks. It was the first time anyone had heard Peiper use the word "fear," and Dietrich dressed him down for it. "Fear" they were tanks, indeed! Find out!

In any event, Peiper said calmly, his plans were already made. At dawn, he would seize the bridge and capture the highway.

CHAPTER TEN

Stavelot, Belgium
18 December

In Andy's dream something had gone terribly wrong.

The Germans had overrun the bivouac area where the squad slept, and Sergeant Nava was rushing about, swearing and kicking his men and ordering them to get up and fight. What made it worse was that the sun had cooled to a black cinder. Blackness suffocated Andy as he threshed in his sleeping bag. Men were panting like dogs and falling around, trying to pull on wet shoes and other men's helmets.

But suddenly he realized that Nava, the Stone Age sergeant, was really kicking them. It was no dream at all!

"Out of there, you idiots! They're on the bridge!"

A match flared; the sergeant transferred the flame to the stub of a candle. All over the cellar, bewildered men collided with each other as they groped for packs and rifles. Through the door swept a snarl of rifle fire and yells. The air quaked with the crash of high-velocity shells. Andy found his glasses and pulled on his shoes, his heart thudding.

"Get the lead out, will you?" Nava roared.

Andy blundered through the command post behind Apache. Panicky signalmen were tearing out the communications rig they had set up a few hours earlier. Outside, the cold fell crushingly. A stone-colored dawn hung over the Amblève River, with coils of black clouds above the bluffs. The firing swelled sharply; a machine gun rattled. Engineers and armored infantrymen streamed from the river up the road toward the town square. Some took shelter behind walls and woodpiles.

A command car howled around the corner and stopped near Andy. An officer beckoned.

"Everybody up to the square! A tank's crossed the bridge."

"Who's going to blow it?" Nava yelled back.

"It's too late! Take off—"

"Too late!" Nava stared at him. *Too late?*

Andy felt the overwhelming weight of the whole German Army—tanks, assault guns, foot soldiers—funneling through that ancient stone bridge into the town. They had had all night; and it had not been blown.

Nava struck his helmet with his fist and looked for someone with whom to share his disbelief. His eyes seized Andy's, almost in accusation.

"Motherogod, what are they *talking* about? They had all night! They let the bastards lift the mines. They didn't use the guns. They didn't blow the bridge!"

A shell exploded blindingly on the roof of a building. Slates peppered the sky and rained down in clinking fragments. The concussion deafened everyone, tore helmets off. Nava came alive. Cursing, he got the men stumbling up the strip of muddy road to the town square. A truck passed, skidding; an ambulance slued by with its rear door banging. Behind sheds and walls, frightened bazooka teams were getting set.

From the river came the jingling clatter if a machine gun. A man beside Andy fell, and he reached down to help him, saw blood spots freckling his cheeks and a sticky mass under the lip of his helmet. He ran on, retching.

They streamed into the marketplace. Men hurried in and out of buildings with weapons and ammunition chests. Trucks were stalled in the square in a hopeless jam. A neat little 3-inch tank destroyer began firing toward the river.

Bewildered, Andy stuck close to Nava. There was no suggestion of a line, no one to report to. He saw the red-cross flag of an aid station flapping before a shop. Some officers jumped from a car and ran into a small stucco hotel.

Suddenly a salvo of 88 shells whistled over. He hurled himself down, with the rest of the squad, but the shells fell high on the upper slope of the town. The troops in the square ran about still more frantically, knowing that succeeding salvos would drop in the square. Another tank destroyer began to crack.

"Get up, idiots!" Nava ordered. He vaulted into a truck, skidding supplies back to the tailgate. The squad lifted out two light machine guns and crates of ammunition. Andy laid a machine-gun tripod across his shoulder. Jumping down, Nava took a machine gun under his arm, and assigned loads.

The squad straggled toward the buildings lining the south side of the marketplace. Pop's face was purple with strain. He stumbled to his knees. Two men got him going again.

Nava opened the door of a building whose old brick walls were the color of dried blood. He peered inside, a grenade palmed for throwing. A Belgian in an overcoat nervously beckoned them in. Nava charged past him. *"Kommen sie—"*

Andy stumbled into what looked like a small factory. Empty display cases lined the walls of a small, dark salesroom. A door opened on a workroom. From upstairs he heard a wild racket of rifle shots. They thundered up the stairway and emerged into a loft with ancient machinery bolted to the floor and power belts sagging across the ceiling. Andy saw riflemen kneeling at the windows. Every window was manned, and Nava headed up the last flight of stairs. They came out in a dark hall. Nava moved along, kicking doors open and assigning a man or a team to each room. He put Pop and Rotunno in a room that had taken a hit in some previous battle. Blown out almost to floor level, the wall provided a parapet low enough for the machine gun.

Next to it, in another shell-damaged room, he and Andy set up the second machine gun. As they worked, he muttered to himself:

". . . All night to blow the bridge, and they didn't even— Abe, that old man's gonna die of heart failure. Come on, baby, *operate!*" pulling savagely at the bolt. "Croft! Are you lookin' for targets?"

Andy adjusted his glasses, his nerves faltering. He cringed at what he saw. Hopeless! His glance raced down the slope over ground cluttered with buildings, trees, wagons, sheds. At the bottom, the slope fell into the icy blackness of the river. A King Tiger inched over the ancient stone bridge, filling it rail to rail. Behind it crept an impatient line of military traffic. Gray forms slipped among the vehicles, crowded past the tank, ran to cover on the north bank.

Nava fired a couple of shots to clear the action.

Andy pointed out the infantrymen on the bridge. Squads and teams now ran from building to building. Nava pressed the trigger, and a string of tracers floated away in a slow, graceful arch, falling short of the river. He adjusted the sight, and another burst shocked the ears.

"Get some weight on the feet of this thing."

In the next room, Pop's machine gun started hammering.

Andy swept up an armful of rubble to stabilize the tripod. The sergeant fired back and forth over the bridge, tracers and glinting steel-jacketed slugs floating away. Suddenly three of the figures on the bridge toppled. Like toy soldiers, they lay on the snow. Another fell; then a heap of running men went down.

The soldiers behind tried to turn back. Officers in command cars threatened them with pistols. They climbed over the bodies and rushed forward into the streams of bullets. A dozen fell. Others leaped the rail and scuttled under the bridge.

Andy closed his eyes as the Tiger rolled over the bodies. Then he heard an incoming shriek, a roar, and felt the building rock. Bricks and dust cascaded before the window. He looked down the street. A Panther was firing on the run as it charged up hill. He saw flames winking around its machine guns; then its cannon flashed, and a shed beside the road blew into rubble. There were glimpses of a bazooka tube soaring end over end, of bodies flying. Behind the Panther came the Tiger, swarms of soldiers huddling on it. A German assault gun squeezed into an alley and commenced shelling the marketplace.

The roar built up. Plaster fell in great crusts; a strangling dust thickened the firecracker fumes of powder. Andy fell; he was lifted and dropped by shock waves, his helmet rolling on the floor. Ears ringing, he groped for his spectacles.

Then came the brightest flash of all. Light seemed to scald the inside of his skull. There was an earsplitting roar, then silence.

. . . Someone lay beside him. He recognized Nava's voice, but his face was black with powder and dirt. "Are you hit?" he was saying.

Andy saw a brightness in the air, a rind of brilliance out-lining the ragged remnants of the wall. The radiance faded, and pain drilled into his ears.

"Come on, kid—we're pullin' out. The room next to us took a hit. Follow me—"

Andy crawled to his feet. *I followed you and look where I am. I followed my brother, too . . . out of high school, into hell. If I ever get out of this, I'll never follow anybody else the rest of my life.*

In the hall, men were coughing in the dust. Andy groggily leaned against the wall. Vague shapes came and went. From the marketplace rang a clamor of screams and explosions. It was as though a giant fireworks stand were going up, cre-mating the clerks and customers.

Andy glanced into the next room, where Pop had been. Faint daylight leaked in over a smashed machine gun. There was no sign of Pop and Vito, only their helmets in the rubble, and scraps of cloth. The walls looked as though a bag of ripe plums had burst in the room. He gagged, and began to sob.

Nava yelled at him to move. They were running and fall-ing down the stairs. Outside, medics were carrying litters into a building. A cold sleet blew. Andy saw trucks roaring off up the highway toward the woods above town. A truck, its can-vas top frosted with snow, was parked before the building, and a lieutenant was herding men into it.

"Let's go! All aboard—"

Nava started helping his men over the tailgate into the truck, which was already creeping forward. The lieutenant yelled a warning at the driver, and it halted. As soon as the squad was in, he mounted behind them. There was scarcely breathing room in the crowded six-by-six truck. As it lurched away, Andy was thrown back against Apache. He braced himself for the right-angle turn toward the foothills, but the truck continued straight ahead. Puzzled, he looked out the back. A double line of buildings closed in behind them. The marketplace receded. All the traffic he could see was turning north toward the hills. But they, for some reason, were following the paved road west down the river.

Nava hitched toward the young lieutenant, his grimy face alarmed. "Lieutenant! We're going the wrong way."

"No, we're going to Trois Ponts," the lieutenant said vaguely.

"What for?"

"Orders. I—I'm supposed to set a roadblock there. Most of that German column will be following us. They've crossed to the north side of the river to get on the pavement, you see. Now they'll have to cross back to keep heading west. The river turns north at Trois Ponts."

Nava stared at him, his features ugly. "So we're going to blow the bridge and set a roadblock, huh?"

The young officer, chewing his lip, nodded silently.

"Will you tell me—sir—what's the use of wiring bridges when they don't get blown anyway?" Nava demanded.

The lieutenant clung to a top support as the truck roared along. "I guess our mistake was in placing troops across the river last night. The Germans captured our guns this morning before we knew what was going on. We couldn't blow the bridge until our men got back across, you see—"

"Oh, I see, all right! I see that I lost two men because you jokers didn't blow the bridge. And now we'll play the game all over again at some other bridge."

The lieutenant kept chewing his lip. He looked not over twenty years old, and Nava finally settled back and asked disgustedly:

"Have we got *anything* at this place we're going to? Troops? Weapons?"

"I don't know," the lieutenant said hoarsely. "I haven't the faintest idea. I had charge of a map section in Stavelot, you see, until last night—"

Nava glanced at Andy with an expression of despair. "Maps!" he muttered. He closed his eyes and swayed in a semicoma of exhaustion. All the strength suddenly bled out of Andy too, as the immediate fear that had been his support leaked away. In his mind there was no doubt that they were all going to die today. Their number was up. Vito's and Pop's deaths proved the squad's luck had run out. Yet he thought: The hell with it—get it over with. While, deep inside him, a tiny pilot light flickered stubbornly. When the time came, he knew he would go through the motions again till he dropped.

For a few minutes the truck wound along a narrow, paved highway, the river visible a few hundred yards to the south. In a deathlike languor, Andy gazed out at the frozen marshlands along the Amblève. Little forested hills stood up, and deserted farms were neatly tucked into the woods.

Suddenly the brakes squalled, and someone in the cab pounded on the window.

"Roadblock!"

"Oh, my God!" the lieutenant moaned.

As the truck stopped, Nava sang out, "Hit the ditches!"

Sprawling into the ditch, Andy grabbed a quick glimpse of the terrain ahead. The road sloped down to a railroad overpass. A couple of dozen men who had been laying mines were running to cover in some heather-like growth beside the road. He worked the bolt of his M-1 and tried to pull a bead on one of the men. The lieutenant knelt near him with binoculars to his eyes.

Nava jumped up.

"What the hell, Lieutenant, they're GI's! Let's go, before something catches up with us."

The lieutenant ordered everyone into the truck again, standing on the running board as they proceeded. Presently Andy heard him pipe: "Hold your fire, soldiers! Americans!"

"Stay put," Nava said as the truck stopped, and he swung over the tailgate. Andy raised the canvas side cover and watched GI's rising from the frozen plants beside the road. A lieutenant in a muddy combat jacket crawled from the ditch, white-faced and scared. He ran toward the truck.

"What's the scoop?" he panted.

"Stavelot just fell to the Germans!" shouted the other lieutenant. "My CO ordered me down here to blow a bridge."

"There's *three* bridges! We're wiring them as fast as we can."

The officers were now standing six feet apart but still bellowing at each other.

"Let's get going with those mines!" Nava ordered the soldiers standing on the road. They jumped, and started swinging mattocks against the concrete roadway. Antitank mines lay along the way. Andy saw sparks fly as the mattocks rang futilely on the cement. The job appeared hopeless.

"How many men you got here, Lieutenant?" Nava asked.

"We're about a company strong—51st Combat Engineers. They sent us up from near St. Vith last night. We just got the word to blow the bridges. What the hell's coming?"

"Armor—infantry—you name it!" the other lieutenant said. "Where should I report?"

Andy let the curtain fall back. He looked at Apache, at

Leo, at the other Lions. Everyone was shaking. Was the damned Army ever ready for anything? On the third day of a retreat, couldn't a few bridges be ready to dynamite before the enemy arrived?

He heard the lieutenant shouting at the driver to drive on, as Nava crawled in over the tailgate. The truck rumbled past the soldiers chipping at the concrete road surface. Nava raised the side curtain as they roared through the underpass and climbed to a ridge above a shallow river valley.

Andy saw two rivers flowing together in a big Y below them. One of them was the Amblève, sweeping north in a half-circle to trap the highway in a loop. The other river, a smaller one, came up from the south to its rendezvous with the Amblève. Their muddy waters met and flowed north into a jumble of rough, wooded hills.

The highway turned left to cross the Amblève by a flimsy-looking Army bridge, then ran on a few hundred yards to a second bridge over the other river. Andy saw the town of Trois Ponts on the far side of the rivers.

They passed an antitank cannon beside a ruined stone house. Four artillerymen were pitching up clods to make a protective lunette. Near the river, the road forked, a muddy branch of it following the Amblève north. The truck turned toward the bridge. The blast of its exhaust shook the windows of a little cluster of buildings at the approach to the bridge. Along the street, at intersections, Engineers were setting up machine guns and lugging bazooka rounds into alleys. They hurried on. Andy was praying to cross the bridge and keep going.

A large sign loomed beside the cobbled street:

YOU ARE CROSSING THE AMBLÈVE RIVER
Courtesy 291st Engr C Bn

The bridge looked as though it had been built by second-rate spiders out of scrap cobwebs, he thought; but between its frail side supports lay sturdy metal floorplates. Frantic GI's were crawling all over it with yellow wire and crates of TNT.

A noncom questioned the driver and waved them across.

With a shudder, Andy peered down at the current flowing cold and muddy beneath the bridge, a rim of ice gleaming along the banks.

"Did you see them Belgians peeking out of the houses?" Worden said. "Lousy Kraut-lovers! Bet they tip them off to where every gun's placed."

They crossed a wedge of land and slowed for the crossing of the second bridge. Downriver, Andy saw a third one. The key bridge, he saw now, was the first, for without jumping back across the Amblève, the Germans were not going anywhere.

A second sign said:

YOU ARE CROSSING THE SALM RIVER
Courtesy 51st Engr C Bn

Built by funny Engineers, back when war was a game, Andy thought bitterly. The truck crept across and up a stone street into the town. Blocks of business buildings and little hotels faced the river. He saw signs in German and French. Beyond the town loomed forested hills.

An officer ran from one of the hotels, and there was a shouted discussion of where to post the lieutenant's men. The officer finally said:

"Leave a third of the men at the far side of this bridge. Take the rest back to the first bridge. If we don't destroy it, we've at least got to hold them long enough to blow the second—"

The men groaned as the truck recrossed. Andy held his

head in his hands. From heaven to hell in one jump, he thought dismally.

At the roadblock, the lieutenant from Stavelot, in an attack of command fever, began choosing men. "You men on this side of the truck get out—I'll keep you here. Sergeant, take charge of the rest. Get them to that first roadblock, on the double—"

Andy and several of the Lions started to rise, but Nava said sharply:

"As you were! What'samatter, Lieutenant, didn't that OCS vaccination take?"

The lieutenant reddened. "I don't know what you mean," he muttered.

Andy knew, and he knew the lieutenant knew. There was something about an officer being willing to do anything he asked of his men. The lieutenant was playing safe.

"Forget it," Nava said. "But I got a working combat squad here, the only one in Belgium as far as I know. There's no sense in breaking it up."

"All right! The hell with it! Leave me a third of the men and take off."

The lieutenant hurried away.

"Tough luck, doughs," Nava muttered, as the truck lurched on to the other bridge. "It ain't the best spot in Europe, but the main idea is to get the job done. And you oughtta know by now that no Engineer can be trusted."

On the far side of the Amblève, they rolled back into the congregation of narrow two-story structures clustered near the bridge. They must have been built by cake decorators working in stone, Andy decided—solid little buildings larded with ornamentation. Ammunition was being carried into some. At an intersection, two men with a bazooka lay behind a low mound of rubble. A block beyond, another bazooka team was digging in.

The truck stopped. A man with a master sergeant's chevrons on his helmet ran around to the rear as Nava jumped out. He was carrying a handie-talkie.

"Whattayou got?" he demanded.

"Fifteen heads," Nava said.

"Any bazookas or .50 calibers?"

"No. Where do you want us at?" Nava said tersely.

"Any bazookamen?" asked the master sergeant.

Andy shrank into his overcoat with a glance at Leo.

"Croft—Miles!" Nava said.

Andy and Leo dropped to the street and stood dejectedly near the sergeants.

"There's a bazooka team down at the next corner," said the sergeant, "that I'd hate to trust with a water pistol. They were off-bearers in a sawmill till last night. Take over from them. I got one heavy machine gun in the same block and a lookout in the steeple of the church. I gotta stay near the bridge, so if you'll take charge down here, Sergeant—"

"Nava," said Nava, extending his hand.

"Grimm," said the other. They shook.

"If you can knock off one of them Tigers for me, we'll have time to blow the bridge. I'm counting on that AT gun doing it, actually."

While the men were crawling from the truck, a red flare went up from the church a quarter of a mile away. Sergeant Grimm tuned in his handie-talkie, and a wild voice rasped out, "They're coming!"

Grimm said: "Post your men, Nava, and get everybody the hell out of sight!"

Leo and Andy were led to a tiny corner store. Nava ran off. The small windows had been crisscrossed with adhesive tape to prevent glass flying. One of the windows had been knocked out to provide a vantage place. Andy kept thinking of those poor antitank gunners near the underpass. He saw them with their little gun, naked and helpless in the face of the German Army. Nava came back to make a final check on them.

"You know the deal," he said. "Go for their tracks. If you cripple one, lay a smoke shell into the turret and they may think they're afire."

Whannng!

The first shot in what must be a short-lived duel echoed from the railroad underpass. A second explosion crossed its echoes. Nava ran out.

There was a rapid series of loud reports from the highway: three fired shots, three hits. "Them poor bastards!" Leo moaned.

Whannng!

"They're still firing!" Andy said.

There was more tank fire—high-velocity shells hurled by bold men in iron foxholes. Machine guns rattled. Then a mighty explosion quaked the air, followed by a crumpling of burning ammunition.

"They got one! They got one!" Leo yelled.

Andy pictured a Tiger blown up in the cramped underpass. It would have to be dragged back by another tank with a towing cable.

Whannng! Whannng! Whannng!

The antitank crew was still blasting away. More 88's picked up the challenge. Explosions rocked the village. Nava ducked in.

"The lookout counts nineteen tanks on the road," he told them. "One of them is burning in the underpass. Those idiots on the bridge still aren't ready with their charges."

"Sarge!" Andy blurted. "How about letting a tank pass and going for its ammunition rack?"

"Negative," Nava said. "It's not that easy to hit, and by the time it's passed, another tank will be firing down your throats. I figure we'll get the bridge wired up in time, but if we have to bivouack, here's the deal: Crawl out one of the side windows and take off. Turn right at the first corner, to the Café Lienne. I've made reservations," he added, with a wink. "A Belgian came to me and said he's got a cellar we can use. Take off, if you get a chance. Good luck, Lions. Meeeow!"

For fifteen minutes the incredible duel at the underpass roared on. The little AT gun yapped spitefully at the mastodons in its front yard. But suddenly the firing ceased. Tank engines growled and barked like bulldogs.

Andy felt like crying. The antitank gun had been knocked out. Brave guys . . . And now they were scraps of bloody uniform in the snow and mud.

Five minutes later the clash of track plates echoed along the little street. Scraping sounds told of a tank making room for itself between the stone curbs. All at once a reverberating explosion shook the building. Some windows broke. Andy saw a pink-and-blue flash reflected in the glass across the street. *What goes on?* he thought wildly. He heard debris falling—stone, boards, clanging metal—and in the echoes of it all, a faint cheering.

They looked out. The bridge had gone. Andy went cold all over. Where it had stood, he saw the butt ends of timbers rising from the muddy water. On the spit of land beyond, trucks were rolling toward the bridge over the Salm.

Leo began to cry and curse.

"They left us! Didn't even give us a chance!"

An odd weakness hit Andy in the knees. He had to move, had to run. Climb out a window, Nava had said, and run to the first corner. But he felt dizzy and hollow. His knees were rubber. He was cold and faint. On the walks, he heard GI's running, yelling at one another. There was a long, sustained rattle of machine-gun fire from a block away. A man screamed. Something like a heavy parcel fell in the street.

Leo dropped the bazooka. The clang of the tube on the floor jarred him loose. Terror vomited up through him like a black upwelling of blood.

"Let's go!" Leo screamed. He was clearing jagged stalagmites of glass from the window frame with his gunbutt. Then he stepped through, and the sound of his boots faded along the walk. The tank noises swelled. A shell shrieked in and exploded in the street. Flying slivers of steel smashed out half the windows on one side of the room.

Andy crawled through the window and ran after Leo, slipping and sliding on the frozen walk. At the corner, Leo slipped and fell, scrambled up, and ran out of sight to the right. Andy followed, gasping. He heard the first tank passing, machine guns yammering.

Down the block three men swerved into view. Andy halted. They too halted, seeing him and Leo. But all were GI's and all ran on until the three other men turned in at a doorway. Leo plunged after them. Andy entered the Café Lienne as a Belgian in hat, overcoat, and muffler was telling them:

"À bas, messieurs! À bas! C'est à dire—"

The soldiers were Shanks, Apache, and Worden. "What's he sayin'?" Shanks panted, as Andy rushed in.

"I don't know. *Sprechen sie Deutsch?*" he asked the Belgian.

"*Ja! Im keller, macht schnell!*"

"In the cellar!" Andy said, pushing at them as the café owner led to the rear.

The café was small and dark, with a little bar, many-paned windows, and ancient nineteenth-century furniture. They clattered down a winding staircase lit by a single hung lantern, to emerge into a cellar smelling of wine and hams. Empty meathooks festooned the ceiling, which was the floor of the upper room. Bottles were stored in racks; beer kegs and wine kegs were cradled along the walls. From far off there was a rising thunder of shelling. The tank column was throwing a temper tantrum. A thought ran across his mind half noticed, like a mouse:

We stopped them! We stopped them!

"Oh, hell, they'll find us here!" Shanks groaned. "First place they'll look is the cellars."

But the Belgian was grappling a wine keg from its place against a wall. He moved some boards from behind it, and pointed.

"Another room!" he beamed. "Since 1940, when they came the first time. There are candles."

The men began crawling inside. Worden hesitated. "I hope this guy ain't a Kraut lover. I knew some Belgians in Brooklyn—"

"You aren't in Brooklyn, Sam," Andy snarled. "And this man is risking his life to hide us, so get your tail in there!"

But Worden still hesitated. "What happens when they haul these barrels off? They won't be here long, buddy."

Andy asked the Belgian, who gestured. "The wine is spoiled! The other kegs will go first."

"Danke! Viele danke!" Andy said.

"I ask one favor. Please take care of the cat. His name Monsieur Léopold, like mine."

"Monsieur Léopold, many thanks. Will you keep an eye out for our sergeant?"

"Ja. If there is danger, I thump three times on the floor."

The cellar was snug, and as soundproof as a cave.

The walls were of crudely laid stone. Three surprisingly sound bunks, stacked one atop the other, spanned one wall. They found a box of candles, and used a couple to inspect their shelter. The length of one wall was lined with paintings, bric-a-brac, a sofa, and boxes of family possessions. Worden reached up to pat the top bunk. Something hissed. He leaped back.

"What the hell!"

"That's the cat," Andy said.

"I hate cats," Worden said bitterly.

"You don't like Belgians, either, but you'll love this one and his cat, or you're out in the cold.—Listen!" Andy dropped his voice to a whisper.

Boots pounded the ceiling.

"Blow out the candles!" someone said.

Footfalls clumped down the cellar stairs. Wine kegs scraped beyond the wall. Then a voice asked, "Any Lions in there?"

The tension went down like steam pressure. Nava crawled in. The boards were rearranged by someone outside; candles were lighted, and they saw Nava sitting with his back to the wall, grinning.

"Oh, Mother! Them Jerries are walking up the walls! They'll be fighting each other pretty soon."

"I'd like to fight me a couple of Engineers," Leo said. *"Now* what do we do?"

"We sit tight," Nava said. "The Engineers didn't have time to warn us. If they had, we'd've been gunned down in the street anyway. They did good to blow that bridge."

"Where's the other guys?"

"Sergeant Grimm took 'em down the river. He hopes to find another bridge, a little one his bunch saw on the way up from St. Vith."

"Wonder if there's some grub here," Apache said.

They searched. Under the sofa they found a metal canister half filled with oatmeal, a case of red wine, and some coarse sugar in a linen sack.

"Wine!" Leo said. "I got so sick on wine once—"

"You better not get sick on this wine, soldier—not in these quarters," Nava warned.

He doled oatmeal into their mess kits, crumbled a little sugar onto it, and added water. Then he poured a little wine into each man's canteen cup.

Suddenly, in the café, feet shuffled and voices resounded. Someone thumped three times on the floor. Nava started blowing out candles.

German voices came in a steady mutter as furniture was shifted. There was a bad moment when what sounded like a full squad of soldiers checked out the cellar. Kegs were moved, bottles clinked. A German baritone began to bray:

"Horch, vas komm' von Drauss und Rhein—!"

Other voices joined in. Singing like a glee club, the searchers ascended the stairs, and the cellar was silent.

Andy's watch showed 1730 when Nava struck a match. He lit two candles. "You can whisper, but hold it down," he warned. "They must be using the café for a command post."

In silence they ate, then unrolled packs and changed socks. The cat went to the crawl hole, sniffed and scratched at it, then began trying optimistically to excavate a small hole in the flagstone floor.

"What's the idiot doin'?" Worden asked.

Nava sighed. "What we'll all be doing pretty soon. We'd better start digging a certified clean rest room while they're still clattering around upstairs."

They raised flagstones and dug beneath them with entrenching tools. The loose earth was then packed under the sofa. When the hole was three feet deep, they let Léopold test it, threw in a little dirt, and arranged flagstones across it.

Andy saw that everyone felt good about the latrine. It stood as proof that they were going to be safe here for a long time. It was like laying a cornerstone for a new bank.

After an hour they ate another ration of oatmeal. With oatmeal in his whiskers, wine on his breath, Nava muttered:

"Four bunks, six men. Four of you will sleep at a time; the others will stand watch and keep each other awake. Sleep face down to cut down the danger of snoring."

At 1900, a man descended the cellar steps. By his cautious tread, Andy guessed that it was Monsieur Léopold—no hobnails, no swagger. The keg was moved; the boards slid aside. Andy knelt by the hole. Monsieur Léopold's face showed.

"They send me for wine," he whispered. "Here is food." He pushed some cheese and a round black loaf of pumpernickel bread into the shelter. "They are using my café as headquarters. Twenty-two villagers were massacred in the streets! Bloody SS swine!"

"God!" Nava said, as Andy translated. "And he'll be Number Twenty-three if they find us. Tell him—tell him we understand that," he said humbly. "And we appreciate it."

Andy thanked Monsieur Léopold. The Belgian's eyes sparkled with tears and fire. "If you have a map," he said, "please let me borrow it. I will mark what I see on their maps, and bring it to you every day you are here. It can be a game with you—keeping up with the Boches! We will lay them all in their graves."

CHAPTER ELEVEN

St. Vith, Belgium
20 December

Tom woke slowly and painfully in his foxhole in the woods before St. Vith. Thick, furry flakes of snow had brought an early dusk. He reckoned it must be at least 1900; he had dropped off. All day, the German artillery had pounded the roadblock where the half-starved Americans still straddled the main highway to the west, blocking the Nazi advance. Now the guns had gone silent. He wondered fearfully whether German troops were advancing on the woods for a night assault.

Raising his head, he strained to see beyond the frozen thickets. It was too dark. Everything reminded him of the terrible days in the Monschau Forest, except that the defense here was almost without order.

He could not separate, in his mind, the three days since the first few German tanks blundered into their trap. The first assault units apparently were in no hurry. They had come too far, too fast. But after their support caught up, they began ripping in earnest at the thin American defense lines around St. Vith. Two crashing blows had rolled Tom's battalion back into the woods. All around St. Vith the ring was closing. In the woods, they were waiting now for the end.

Sick and dizzy, hoping food might strengthen him, Tom opened a ration box. His frostbitten fingers were slow; his mind was dead. In his misery, he felt like an old aborigine squatting in a mudhole, waiting for death.

A whistling in the sky brought him to life. Pulses racing, he hurled himself back under the logs that sheltered part of his hole from tree bursts. The assorted misfits in his twenty-man platoon, as Lieutenant Fox called it, were yelling at each other in hoarse panic. Four hurtling, splintering explosions shook the woods. Trees were cracking and falling. The explosions rolled closer; now the men were all calling for him.

"Sarge! I'm movin' back!"

"I think Dixon's hit!"

Tom raised his head, and screamed: "Shut up and keep your heads down! Its gonna get worse before it gets better."

The men were all sick, but he had learned that they could go farther on abuse than on sympathy.

Roaring and flashing, with snow sluicing from tossing branches, the barrage went on. Giant hunks of shrapnel collided with the pines like blind birds. After an hour the shelling lifted. In a few minutes a runner from the company command post came to Tom's trench.

"Your wire's out. The lieutenant wants you."

Tom groaned and sent Rossi, an ex-mechanic, to repair the break while he hurried to the command post. Fox was barricaded in a maze of logged-over trenches with a central room. Tom crawled inside, where, in the blue rays of blackout flashlights, several other noncoms awaited the latest bad news. Collins was a vision of foulness, a Halloween mask of clotted whiskers, dead-black eyes, and dead-white skin.

"Are we pulling out?" Collins asked Fox.

The lieutenant scratched in his underwear. "Not yet, Corp. They aren't even pulling out teeth around here. A new defensive line is being set up behind St. Vith. Sometime tomorrow we'll move back to it. Get your men ready. It might help their morale to know we're going to move."

"I've got two men in their fifties with grandchildren, Lieutenant," Tom said. "They're too far gone to walk out if the order comes."

"They'll have to," Fox said. "In the morning, if the Germans don't assault, I'll call you here one at a time. A scout will show you our escape route. After that, when the order comes, you'll be on your own. —Croft, stay here. I want to talk to you."

The blackout curtain flapped and closed behind the noncoms. Fox lit a cigarette.

"Seventy refugees from 422nd Regiment wandered in just after dark," he said. "They're back at the collecting station. If you want to take a few minutes to see if your brother's with them, go ahead. Then get back to your platoon. If he's there, you have my permission to bring him with you—if he'll come, that is."

It was too dark to run. Tom groped from tree to tree. There was a mysterious reluctance in him to play the scene ahead. To know that Andy had not made it out would be bad enough. To see a shaking, tearful old man of eighteen he might have become would be worse. Tom knew too much about war, now, to imagine Andy's surviving unchanged. In his reveries he always saw a beanpole of a kid, all Adam's apple, oversize helmet, and spectacles, but healthy and eager to please. He did not want his good memories ruined.

Through the dark came voices, moans, glints of light. He leaned against a tree, his face quivering. He crushed his palm against his forehead for control. I'm tired. Tired to the middle of my brain.

In the clearing, dark figures moved over the trampled snow. There was a tent, and near it a row of dead and wounded on litters. Among them stood a craggy figure with the voice of Sergeant Howell, the company sergeant.

"I'm okay! It's only my arm. I can't raise it—watch—"

"Yes, I know. It's called hysteria. Not serious, but you'll have to be evacuated."

"Don't tie that damned tag on me!" Howell raged. "I'm going back to Company. It's like my arm was asleep, that's all—"

Throwing the tag on the snow, the sergeant tramped past Tom and vanished into the woods.

Tom touched the arm of a man with a medic's brassard. "Are there some guys from 422nd here?"

"Yeah. Over yonder by the ambulances."

A silent company of refugees sat on the snow, wolfing rations and drinking hot coffee. "Andy?" Tom croaked. There were muttered words, groans, sighs. "Any of you guys 3rd Battalion?" he asked.

No reply. He saw another group of men crouched between two ambulances. He moved over. "Third Battalion?"

A soldier looked up. "Yeah! We moving back?"

"No, I—I'm looking for my brother. He was in Fox Company—"

The soldier nudged the man next to him. "Hey, Junior. Wasn't you in Fox Company?"

Tom lunged forward. "Junior! Hey, guy! How you doing? Where is everybody?"

Junior Pettis, man least likely to succeed, sixteen if he were a day, fierce, ineffective, and half nuts, glanced up. He looked like eighty-seven pounds of twitches and stares. His eyes had been drained of everything but the memories that seemed to occupy him completely.

"Yo," he muttered.

Tom dropped to his knees and clutched his arm. "Don't you know me? Tom Croft!"

"Slept over by the squad room?"

"That was my brother."

No one paid any attention to the reunion. They were re-united with life, too tired to care about anything else.

"You don't look like Tom Croft," Junior said.

Tom fingered his face—gaunt cheeks, blond beard. "Guess I don't, at that. What happened to you guys, Junior? How'd you get out?"

"Walked. Every night. Every damn night."

"Where were you?"

"They murdered us. All those guys in sheets—"

Tom cringed from the big question. He touched Junior's arm. "Listen, Junior. You know my brother, Andy. Was he with you?"

Fingertips touched the cornsilk of Junior's chin. "I—I think—yeah. Him and Apache."

"Well, is he—"

"They're all dead," Junior said.

Tom squeezed his eyes shut. Don't believe him. He's nuts. But his eyes were wet when he opened them.

"Andy too? Are you sure?"

"Oh, he's dead, all right. They're all dead."

A hot race of blood lifted Tom to his feet. "How do you know? How'd you get away?"

"I hid in the woods till the Germans left. Then I went back to—to help. I saw them. They were dead, all right."

"You crazy bastard! You deserted! You don't even know what happened."

"Jeez, it was terrible," Junior said.

"If anybody'd got out, it wouldn't've been you," Tom

snarled. "You went over the hill. You don't even know what happened to them."

Junior sighed and picked at a cold sore on his nose.

Tom went around asking other men about L Company. But Junior was the sole representative of that forgotten unit. A deserter the only survivor. He would never believe it until he saw the telegram from the War Department.

Through the night the German artillery continued to pound the woods. At daylight the shelling suddenly lifted. The ringing crack of tank fire echoed from the north. Tom listened groggily, his feet throbbing with the pain of trench foot, trying to decide what went on.

A mile to the north, he knew, the wooded ridge was broken by a draw that passed through and behind it. There was a village up there called Wallerode. A secondary road followed down the draw from Wallerode, running all the way to St. Vith. If the defense line cracked at Wallerode, the Germans would roll down the draw and cut off the ridge.

Tom heard measured shots from the American cannon companies. Rumor was that a battery commander had been court-martialed for firing a salvo without permission: ammunition was that low.

Dazed, half deaf from the roar of shells, he staggered out to check his men. He visited the foxholes, questioned the mumbling riflemen, and returned with a head count. It seemed way off, but in his trancelike state nothing quite got through to the little room where his reason slept. All night casualties had been led or littered back to the aid station. He had not even tried to keep count.

Now he had the tally: thirteen left. Bad luck. Better kill another man for luck. Kill that lying creep Junior.

He slumped in his foxhole, worn-out and listless. He knew

he should be doing things, but could not remember just what. The telephone jingled; the lieutenant's voice was high and excited.

". . . to the CP on the double!"

On the double, on the double. What a crock of baby mush! Hurry up and wait. He trudged off through the woods to the command post.

Fox looked at him sharply, then gave him two pills without saying a word. He offered a canteen cup of cold coffee to wash them down.

"Take these. They'll put the stars back in your eyes. The Pfc. here will show you our escape route."

Tom gazed dully at a troll-like soldier in a long overcoat and a dented helmet. He had forgotten all about the pullback. The soldier led him along a trail marked by yellow plastic strips nailed to tree trunks. Tom fell once, and the Pfc. waited patiently while he struggled to his feet.

"We go through a mine field here, so stay the hell on the trail," he mumbled.

The woods ended. They gazed into a wide valley veiled by slow-whirling snowflakes. The clerk pointed to the right.

"Wallerode's there—north. St. Vith's the other way. If you get here and there's no guide, head straight west to the new line."

By the time Tom was back at the foxhole line, the pills had shored him up. He felt, all at once, surprisingly strong and confident. He checked on his men and found most of them too exhausted to understand what he was trying to tell them. One man was having fits of giggles; the others sat like zombies. He went to the CP, got some pills from the lieutenant, and distributed them.

At 1300 the heaviest shelling of all suddenly erupted.

For two hours earth and forest shook under the wild,

rocketing shell bursts. Shock waves tore off helmets and caved in sodden trenches. The outfit's three tanks moved up and deployed beside the road, the almost certain point of attack. The air was so full of shapnel that Tom dared not even leave his foxhole.

The barrage lifted. It was 1500, the Belgian winter dusk already falling. Minutes later, Tom heard motors and shouting. Land mines detonated at the edge of the woods. There was screaming. Machine guns rattled. He came to with a start.

"Everybody up!" he bawled.

The Shermans growled on out of sight. Soon afterward, he heard the hard crack of 88's, then an explosion as a tank's ammunition rack went up. The dusky woods were lit with flashes. Other detonations celebrated the destruction of the other tanks.

He seized the telephone and cranked wildly. It spun free —the line was out. He yelled for a man to take a message to CP. The soldier ran off. Tom knew he would probably never see him again.

A wounded man was crying for help. He crawled out to look for him. Suddenly, far behind the defense line, he heard the tearing shriek of a machine pistol: a German Schmeisser! In *back* of us! he realized, in panic. He gave up hunting the wounded man, and yelled:

"Cowboy! Rossi! Round 'em up and let's go. We're flanked!"

As he collected his gear, he heard tanks coming on the paved road. Tank cannons roared, and the screaming crash of shells rocketed all about the forest.

"Cowboy!" he screamed. "Rossi! Where the hell are you?"

A ragged file of men stumbled from the woods. Cowboy, in the lead, waved his rifle.

"All I could find!"

One of the men, Daniels, was coughing in long, tearing spasms. Yesterday's chest cold was today's pneumonia. Tom looked the file over hopelessly, and almost wept. I might get out of here by myself, but with you soggy relics . . . Get yourselves out! he thought angrily. Don't hang around my neck.

But, in despair he told them: "Stay in line and watch for Krauts."

Through the trees, he saw the logged-over trenches of the command post burning. He swung north to avoid the light. There was no hope now of finding the safe path through the mine field. All around, in the deep woods, he heard fierce fire fights, wild bursts of machine firing, grenades roaring. There was no vestige of a line, only gray uniforms and brown ones blundering around, shooting at anything that moved.

"Daniels—cut out that coughing!" he ordered furiously. "If we tangle with a patrol, I want to hear them first. —Fix bayonets," he added, hopelessly.

Limping, stumbling, they groped through the dark woods with bayonets fixed. The fresh snow gave an illusion of light. Suddenly his heart compressed, as, a few yards ahead of them, he saw two men. He stopped breathing and heard his heartbeats. The men were silhouetted in an aisle in the trees. Apparently they could not see him, and he motioned the squad down. GI's or Germans? He scrutinized the helmets. Wrong! They were flat coal-scuttle shapes.

With held breath, he pulled a grenade and slipped the pin. He tossed it, and heard them scream in fright. Quickly he hurled another, as the first exploded. In the second flash, he saw one German with his hands over his face, the other holding his belly. After a half minute he reached back.

"Gimme your grenades," he told Cowboy. "Daniels, **try to stop coughing!**"

The ground ran up, tilted down, and they stumbled without warning into the open. They had reached the edge of the valley. There was the draw at the bottom; beyond it lay the next ridge and the new defensive line. On a hill to the south, St. Vith burned like a torch.

Lying face down, he studied the ground. Frightened as he was, he could scarcely keep his eyes open. The muscle in Fox's magic lozenges had gone flabby. He wanted to sleep forever.

Daniels's coughing roused him to fury. He swore at the soldier until he quieted, then, heart pounding, studied the valley. The faintly luminous draw appeared deserted. It was about a thousand yards across. The peg shapes he saw might be men or fenceposts, even telephone poles. He clambered up. Swaying there, almost crying with the pain in his feet, he ordered hoarsely:

"Get up, damn you! They're right behind us."

But now that the men were down, they seemed unable to rise. Cowboy staggered up and aided Rossi. Tom helped Daniels. They put one another on their feet like drunks finding their way home.

Minutes later, Tom stepped into a ditch and fell flat. Pain and discouragement sat on his back like a boulder. Cowboy gave him a hand. The ditch he had fallen into ran beside a road. He listened for sounds of danger, but it was useless: his head was too full of the rush of blood in his ears.

They clumped across the road, through another ditch, and up the last slope. "Sarge—can we smoke?" Rossi whispered.

"I'll kill you if you light a cigarette," Tom hissed.

Halfway up the slope, Daniels fell and could not be prodded to his feet. He wheezed loudly. "Feel so—so weak," he gasped. "Listen, Ed. I gotta—gotta have more spuds."

"Get up, man!" Tom urged. "We're almost there."

A coughing fit racked the soldier. "If the rush starts—before we peel 'em—"

"He's out of his head." Cowboy whispered it, out of decency. "He's a cook, you know."

"Take his arm."

They got his arms across their shoulders and staggered on. Suddenly a challenge came from the dark.

"Halt!"

"Okay," Tom mumbled. "Don't know the password, soldier."

"Oh, hell, come on. I can see you."

In the deepest possible pleasure, Tom lay on his back, a galaxy of frozen stars revolving overhead. Like Gulliver, he felt pegged to the ground; but his enemies were in his blood. He felt warm and transfigured.

. . . Transfigured? With sudden clarity he realized that he was dead! His body, with all its miseries, had left him—or he had left it—and what remained was his essence, as pure and clean as the transparent last-year's skin of a snake.

But rough-talking angels tramped about, disturbing heaven. "This bunch here. They're in the way. What am I supposed to do with them?"

The stars swung again, lovely, lovely, no troubles in this paradise. Sunlight in the cut-glass stopper of Mom's vinegar cruet. Beautiful. Andy always tried to figure the sequence of colors, but Tom merely twisted the stopper, and dreamed. Pains in his feet slowed the stars in their gentle coursing.

"Don't back over them, stupid. There! Hold it right there."

Someone was asking him to do something. What a joke! They thought he was still alive! Wonder about Andy—How do you get in touch? Men lifted and slid him into a dark place. Then paradise closed down, and he slept.

Rough movements woke him. He saw light, heard engines. The movements stopped, and there were more hoarse angel voices, some of them cursing, some snoring.

"Hey, Croft!"

He squeezed his eyes shut. Uneasily, he suspected that, if he wished, he could move. He did not want to.

"Croft!" It was Collins's voice.

"What?" Tom said, softly, trying out his immortal vocal chords.

"Nothin'. For a minute I thought you were dead."

"I am dead," Tom said. And frowned in a sudden doubt.

Several men chuckled. Collins gave a sour laugh. "Know what you mean. Ain't this beautiful? Home safe!"

Tom's face puckered. For a moment he meant to cry. Knowing he was not dead, he felt cheated. His body and mind were now revived to pain, sorrow, chagrin. Blood vessels in his feet began trying to burst the seams of his shoes.

"Where are we going?" he asked in a croak.

"Hospital—repple depple. Who knows? Look at them damned goldbricks!"

Tom saw that they were parked beside a road. Traffic roared past, and some of the haggard évacués studied the trucks and jeeps.

"Not one doughfoot in the whole mess," Collins said. "Another bunch of lousy chairborne infantry going back to Paris to shortstop us on supplies."

Another man, lying on his belly on a sidebench, muttered: "Well, they ain't ours. That's 82nd Airborne. And don't kid yourself—they're heading for the line. They look too sick to be going to Paris."

After the traffic had passed, the trucks turned north up the road down which the other column had been running south. In the gray light, Tom peered out mournfully at hills, woods, and little farms along a valley. In the fields, the snow had the blemished gleam of old porcelain. A mile or two farther on, the convoy turned down a dirt road onto what had been a farm. Tents flapped in rows at the far end of the field. A stone house with a flag above the door stood near the road.

Dumped out like sacks of potatoes, the évacués drunkenly ranged themselves in platoon formations. Noncoms, nearly as exhausted as they, shouted orders. A few men immediately lay on the snow, too sick to stand. Seized with a blind dizziness, Tom went to one knee and waited to pass out.

A ridiculous little lieutenant in a shortcoat with flaring skirts, a pistol belted around his waist, a clip-board in his hand, strutted from the house. His pants were stuffed tightly into combat boots so that he looked like an overage messenger boy.

In red-faced fury he addressed them.

"—Want you to *ack* like soldiers, *look* like soldiers, and *stand* like soldiers! This is the U.S. Army! Sergeant Scott— march them to the tents! You, there! Ah want good smart Army marching!"

The good smart marching was ruined by men collapsing.

In midafternoon a more successful formation was held. It was made clear that the commanding officer's name was Schofield; that this was a temporary replacement depot; that the nearest village, Trois Ponts, was four miles north, too far away for passes. In fact, they were only seven miles from the fighting. Those able to return to duty would be shifted to line outfits after examination by medical officers. Those classed as unfit would be transferred to hospitals.

Lieutenant Schofield closed the services by reading the Articles of War, which described punishments for various infractions of military law.

I'm still alive, Tom realized bitterly, and the lousy Army hasn't changed a bit.

CHAPTER TWELVE

In the damp chill of the cellar, Andy lay on the top bunk listening for sounds from the German command post above his head. Below him, the half-frozen members of Team Nava killed time playing cards, cleaning weapons, or dozing. Day by day the cold and inaction had clubbed them into dullness. Into their faces he had seen come the haggard holiness of saints in a medieval religious painting—greenish-white, bloodless, bearded, their eyes sunken in their skulls.

Andy felt emotionally mauled by the buffetings of hope and despair. Every day Monsieur Léopold, their host and protector, carried away Nava's map and returned it with new markings copied from the Nazis' wall maps. The Germans were gaining here; they were stalled there. The American northern shoulder had set like cement. In the south it was equally solid.

But in the center of the line the Nazis had driven thirty-five miles, creating a great tumorous bulge in the battle line. Trois Ponts was near the northern arc of that bulge.

The Germans upstairs suffered from the same wild swings of fortune.

196

A few days ago Hauptmann Heydrick, commanding officer of the small force left behind to occupy Trois Ponts, had shouted in glee:

"A great triumph at Bastogne! The city is surrounded. The Amis must now surrender."

The Germans had roared out "Lili Marlene" and sent Monsieur Léopold to the cellar for wine to drink to the fall of that key city in the south.

But on the following day, there was no singing, only drinking. For their own Colonel Peiper had radioed in desperation from the mountains into which he had stormed looking for another bridge after the bridge at Trois Ponts was blown in his face:

"Must have Otto. Send Otto!"

"Who is this 'Otto,' dear God?" demanded the exasperated Heydrick.

"According to the operation code book, *mein Hauptmann,*" said the radioman nervously, " 'Otto' means 'emergency fuel.' "

Team Nava toasted, in wine and oatmeal mush, the desperation of Battle Group Peiper, strangling in the frozen loops of the Amblève River. Three American forces were slugging at Peiper, and his fuel tanks had gone dry.

And now, on the very day before Christmas, the Germans upstairs were quarreling. Heydrick had berated his staff and pleaded with his superiors by telephone. Then he lost his temper.

"I am not responsible for the decisions of my commanding officer, General! If he has burned his equipment and elected to walk out of the mountains, perhaps it is because someone did not deliver the gasoline he requested!"

There had followed a racket of crates being dragged about,

of boots stamping in and out of the café. Then a long silence fell. Nava paced the floor. What was the score? Were the Germans pulling out?

Abruptly, Andy raised his hand. Two men had just walked into the command post.

Propping himself on one elbow, his ear close to the flooring, he strained to hear every sound. Faintly he detected the chug of engines.

"Well, we have lost," said the commandant's voice.

"It's only a small town," said another man, comfortingly.

"I don't mean Trois Ponts, *Leutnant*. I mean the counteroffensive. Battle Group Peiper was the spearpoint of the whole show, and now it is broken. If only we had crossed here . . . *Lieber Gott. Heraus mit uns!* The damned Amis will eat us for Christmas if we don't hurry."

Andy heard a last clumping of boots, then quiet. He dropped to the floor to pass the news. They rolled packs, and waited.

Two hours later, Monsieur Léopold came to claim his cat, and led them back to the world.

Pallid sunlight broke through the clouds as they emerged into the street. Andy turned his face up to the sky, from which faint warmth fell in a spray of silver. His eyelids grew warm against his eyes, tender and sore from the long darkness. The air was so clean and fresh it hurt his nostrils. In the mountains he heard the snore of planes and the rolling thunderclaps of bombardment.

Nava led them to the bridge. On the way, they looked for mines. But the Germans had left too hurriedly to mine and booby-trap the town. The streets were littered with military trash: empty boxes, spent cartridges, piles of blackening tank shells, a few broken rifles. Across the valley Andy saw Engineers already starting to build a ponton bridge across the Salm.

For a few hours Team Nava ruled the town, a token occupation army. Then an advance guard of trucks and halftracks rolled in. Nava hid everyone in a building, and they watched the traffic pass. He had no idea of getting drafted by some combat outfit, he said. Andy saw light tanks, armored cars, trucks, and towed fieldpieces, all with the insignia of the 30th Infantry Division. For an hour the column streamed past, as it moved up the highway toward Stavelot.

Nava pondered out loud what would happen there. They had known for three days that American forces had retaken the town and blown the bridge. Heydrick had put himself in the old nutcracker, he said. He could not advance, retreat, or cross the river.

By midafternoon, the Engineers had finished a floating treadway for light traffic. Andy watched them start another bridge across the Amblève. Night fell, and they returned dispiritedly to the Café Lienne. They prayed to cross and find themselves on the way to a hospital or replacement depot.

By midmorning of Christmas Day the second bridge was finished, and they crossed over. Scabs of dirty ice floated in the water. Trucks roared by, rocking the pontons like rowboats. Andy felt seasick. Nava led his limping ghost squad into Trois Ponts.

They looked around like tourists.

Things had changed a little. German shells had knocked off some masonry and blown out all the glass in town. Over the doorway of the Engineers' old command post was a new sign:

505 PARA. INF. REGT.

The sergeant settled his helmet and walked into the hotel. Andy winced. Every time Nava went into a building, he came out with worse news than he went in with. They waited nervously, their nerves as sore as their feet. Andy watched a mottled bulk of storm clouds tumble across the sky to extinguish the sun.

Anyway, we'll be in tents or billets, he reassured himself. What's the difference where we are? The difference was that he could no longer believe that anything good could happen to this hard-luck outfit.

Nava emerged. One by one they rose to study his face. His features, whiskered and impassive, revealed nothing. Yet Andy detected a tremendous excitement in him—glints of fire behind closed furnace doors.

"Follow me. Route step," the sergeant said gruffly.

Tramp, stumble, tramp. He marched them to the corner and turned up a hill toward a truck parked in a snowy field. The men moaned and groaned.

"My feet!"

"Where we going?"

They suffered as audibly as recruits at the end of the first long hike. All at once, beyond sight and hearing of the headquarters building, Nava turned his face to the heavens and vented a gorilla roar. He beat his breast as they gaped at him. He grinned at them, half brute, half deity.

"Lions, we done fought our war! Now we travel!"

"Where to?" Andy asked. Feeling weak, he leaned against a building.

"They're holding a reunion of old Lions down south of here. We'll catch a ride at the motor pool up yonder. Take L-16 to Lammerding Crossroads, the man said. Or was it Dammerling? Then catch a ride west on M-49. You know what M-49 is, don't you?"

They did not.

"The paved road from Schlausenbach, our old regimental town, to St. Vith and points west!"

Leo whined, "But ain't they fightin' down south?"

"Not where we're going. Somewhere along M-49 we'll run into MP's and get passed back to a collection point. Tents, beds, showers! Then we go back to hospitals or wherever the hell they decide."

He pulled a bottle of Monsieur Léopold's wine from his coat, took a pull at it, and led them on to the motor pool.

I'll believe it when it happens, Andy thought. We weren't going into combat in the Schnee Eifel, either, and look at us now.

But they were traveling within an hour in a random catch of other orphans of the battlefield. Andy rocked on the bench. Wind clawed at the canvas top. Beside the road the hills lay chill and dark.

"The bastard engine is missing," Leo complained, after a half hour. "Wouldn't it be our luck to have to carry the thing on a stretcher?"

Andy listened. He heard a staccato crackling, as of popcorn when the whole panful of kernels begins to burst at once—a prolonged stuttering volley. But this, he realized, was small-arms fire. A fire fight was going on somewhere in the hills.

Nava frowned, then cleared his brow.

"Just some skirmishing. The line's still fluid. We'll turn west in a mile or two. Be out of here in a hurry."

Sunk in exhaustion and despondency, Andy felt a sense of doom, seeing himself as an animal with its leg in a trap, a creature that had struggled so long, so frantically, that nothing was left of its fight. Only the trap was left, and a poison-ous residue of hopelessness. Whatever lay ahead, he knew he had left the last of his strength, his courage, his will, scattered in morsels along the roads of the Ardennes. . . .

CHAPTER THIRTEEN

Near Lammerding, Belgium
25 December

In midmorning Lieutenant Schofield called a formation. The weather had improved. Through holes in the clouds the sunlight fell coldly on the snow-covered ground of the camp. From not far off came the roar of planes. The lieutenant strode from the farmhouse, swatting his thigh with his little swagger stick. A pine branch let fall its load of snow with a swish. Schofield pivoted, as though to put the tree on report.

Tom peered at him through swollen eyes. Even now, days after evacuation, he was still dizzy and nervous. It sometimes seemed to him, however, that the sickest inmate of the camp was the commandant.

"Report!" shouted First Sergeant Scott.

The noncoms reported.

Present or accounted for were eighteen ailing soldiers, all that remained of the original évacués and the scores who had wandered in later. Every day, trucks had rumbled in with the scrapings of the battlefield—sick, lost, or wounded. Every time a truck came in, Tom hurried out to look for Golden Lion shoulder patches. He found a few, but none from Fox Company.

Every day trucks carted off loads of sad-sack GI's earmarked "return to duty." Now the last of the barrel had been scraped. There remained only the sick and the hurt, tagged by medical officers for transfer to hospitals.

Lieutenant Schofield apparently had called the formation today to read a news release.

Battle Group Peiper, he read, trapped in the Amblève River Valley, had burned its equipment and was attempting to march out, leaving hundreds of casualties in the snow.

In the south, the besieged city of Bastogne expected to greet relief columns within twenty-four hours.

The turning point in the Battle of the Bulge had been reached, the lieutenant announced.

However, in a minor line-shortening maneuver, he added, this particular sector was to be abandoned immediately. Startled, Tom and Collins looked at each other.

To make the operation clear, Lieutenant Schofield raised his left arm and extended his right.

"I will demonstrate this maneuver as follows. My left arm represents the line from Trois Ponts to Vielsalm, just south of us. My right arm represents the line turning west from Vielsalm to the Meuse River. You can see that by running a string from my left hand directly to my right hand, our line could be greatly shortened."

The inmates saw that. What they did not see was what happened to them, isolated down around his belt buckle.

"This camp," said the lieutenant, "will therefore be inactivated pursuant to orders from Corps Headquarters. . . ."

The news hit Tom a sudden, surprising blow. He was about to leave behind any hope of Andy's coming in someday with another bunch of refugees. Soon the enemy would roam this area as they now swarmed through St. Vith.

As they rolled packs, he said: "I can't see my brother dead, you know? I mean, it wouldn't happen to a guy like him."

Deadpan, Collins finished rolling his blankets.

"He spoke good German," Tom continued. "So they'd have had him back at Regimental Headquarters doing interrogation, or—you know—something like that. Right?"

Collins buckled his blanket roll into the pack carrier, muttering at a short strap.

"He was so *bright*," Tom went on. "He wouldn't let himself get in a spot where he'd just be lugging a rifle, not using his talents." He frowned. "I mean—he *is* bright, not—not *was*. . . ."

Collins savagely swore at the pack strap.

"It makes sense, doesn't it?" Tom pleaded.

Collins gave a sigh. "If it makes sense to you, soldier, that's all that matters."

It did not make sense, though. Grief came down over Tom like a collapsed tent. The pain he had staved off with self-delusion now ripped his flesh with the ragged hurting power of a tin-can lid. He bent over his pack to hide the tears that suddenly flooded his eyes. But a sob choked him. He hoped Collins had not heard. He cleared his throat to cover it.

Collins said: "Don't want a butt, do you? I bummed a couple off Sergeant Scott."

Tom shook his head.

Collins struck matches until he found one dry enough to catch fire.

"We shoulda swiped a coupla bottles of the loot's applejack. Sure could use a drink. Tell you one thing. When you and me hit Paris, we're gonna get fixed up for the rest of *this* war!"

Collins began breaking down the Army cot. Then he said:

"I ain't knocking what you said, buddy. He could come walking in here right now, and I wouldn't be surprised. The whole 106th Division had to come out through Vielsalm, like it was a funnel. But I wouldn't be surprised if he'd got captured, either. Or killed. Because—let's face it—we ain't exactly on maneuvers in Tennessee."

Tom nodded, somehow grateful to Collins for expressing what he knew.

They rolled the frozen tents. The sky darkened like a bruise, and the wind strengthened. As they finished, two trucks rolled in to haul them to their new posts.

Lieutenant Schofield's gear had already been piled in the jeep. He passed to the front of the group and stood facing it. Drivers wearing the shoulder patch of 7th Armored Division waited beside the trucks.

"Attention, men," the lieutenant said, with a smile. "Commend you all for your attitude. You're wearing your medical evacuation tags? Very good. Turn them in as I pass before you—danger of their being lost. They will precede you—"

Collins was as suspicious as a watchdog, but when he gave up his tag, Tom surrendered his also.

With a roar of engines, chain-shod treads chomping at the road, the trucks pulled out.

"So long, you crumby ninety-day wonder!" Tom muttered, making a thumb gesture toward the lieutenant, who lingered in his jeep.

"Hang up your Christmas stocking, Sam—we'll fill it for you," Collins said savagely.

South they rolled a half mile, then west. They were running out along the lieutenant's right arm, now; must be somewhere near his elbow, Tom reckoned. The men lolled on their rolled packs, limp with relief. Some slept. Others smoked. There was no sign of Lieutenant Schofield behind them. Tom closed his eyes, and dozed.

When the trucks slowed, he suddenly heard the sounds of a

fire fight: small-arms fire, gut-shaking roars. The action was on a forested ridge to the south.

The trucks were stopping. Collins and Tom blinked at each other. Tom stuck his head out the back and looked around.

They were at another depressing crossroads: bombed-out plaster ruins, arthritic trees, some dead cows in a field. At the roadside was a tilted signpost: LAMMERDING. Stenciled Army postscripts had been nailed below the town name:

M-49. Tros Ponts. Malempré.

Sleepily, he gazed around. The paved road ran out of sight into the west. He peered south. The crossroad climbed over a mile of tilted, frozen farmland; then hills bucked up under it, and the road vanished into another black forest. He could see the smoke of artillery shells along the crest of the ridge.

"What's goin' on?" Collins asked drowsily.

Tom saw First Sergeant Scott dismount to talk to a young officer in a greasy field jacket, muddy pants, and paratroop boots. Against a stone wall were parked a truck and two anti-aircraft quads on half-track carriers. A captured German self-propelled gun resembling a flimsy tank idled on the road, exhausts steaming. Twenty or thirty troops were warming themselves at a fire of broken timbers.

"I don't know what's up," Tom said slowly, "but Scott's talking to some lieutenant."

Collins sat up with a grunt. All the sleeping men were awake now, owlish and solemn. Tom heard the lieutenant say:

". . . I'll have the whole picture when my scouts get back. According to radio signals from the task force, the Germans haven't been able to get any artillery pieces over to this side of the ridge. Major Rogers says he finally got permission to withdraw his task force, but now he's encircled."

Tom felt a slow icing up of the gut, a premonition, a chilling draft of horror.

Sergeant Scott coughed in embarrassment. "Sir, I wonder if you're confusing us with—"

The lieutenant scanned the hills through binoculars.

"The shells you see landing are being lobbed from across the ridge. The Krauts can't really lay down a barrage for fear of shelling their own men on this side. So if we get in fast, we'll only have infantry to cope with."

Tom's heart froze.

"Lieutenant," said the sergeant, "these here men—"

"The Army way!" said the lieutenant in disgust. "Nobody would assume responsibility for letting Rogers pull his task force out. They wanted him to maintain the roadblock while our line was shortened. So there he sits. They forgot him! I picked up his signal as we were traveling through. I'm anti-aircraft, actually, but what the hell! I can deflect my quads for ground laying and cut those storm troopers off at the knees. And I borrowed a load of riflemen that came along a few minutes ago."

"Yes, sir," Scott said anxiously. "But, sir, this here is a convoy of sick men! We've been in a repple-depple up the line. We're all tagged for a rest area. The CO told me these trucks would take us to Liège."

Dead quiet. Tom held his breath in an ecstasy of suspense.

"Aren't you the men I requested from Team McHenry?"

"No, *sir!* Not us. Didn't reckon there was any combat troops left in our sector."

"What about it, driver?" the lieutenant called to one of the men at the fire. Some wore triangular armored-force shoulder patches, Tom saw. Others, the bulk of them, were muddy, unshaven, spectral-looking infantrymen. The sergeant who had led the trucks here faced the lieutenant, with reluctance.

"Well, sir, I couldn't find Team McHenry," he said, "so when I saw this repple-depple, I asked the CO if he could spare some men for a special, er—detail—"

The lieutenant shook his head. Then: "If you're évacués, Sergeant, where are your tags?"

"The CO took them. For safekeeping, he said."

"Sergeant," the lieutenant said, "I am sorry as hell. But we'll have to do the best we can. It may already be too late to break the ring, but we're going to try. It's hell, but that's what Sherman said war was all about. You may as well unload your men and let them warm up while we wait for the scouts to come back. I'm Lieutenant Hammond, and I'm taking you over."

While the men dismounted, arguing with anyone who would listen, a master sergeant walked from the fire to speak to the lieutenant. Tom saw a 2nd Division Indian Head patch on his overcoat. He was a grim, bearded man who looked as though he had crawled across Belgium under barbed wire: clearly an infantryman, plainly a line sergeant.

"What's the score, Lieutenant?" he asked. "My men are in lousy shape, and the only weapons we've got are small arms."

In what was now old habit, Tom reconnoitered shoulder patches among the men at the fire. Lion heads. Huh! he thought, only half aware. Hundred-and-six. Full-face lions, looking like bronze heads on a wall above a lily pool, the kind that squirted water through their teeth.

He plodded toward the fire, shivering. One of the soldiers looked at him, studying his shoulder patch; curiously at first, then in shock. The soldier was tall and very thin. A week ago he might have been young. His long nose was red with cold, and a pair of GI glasses rode it, patched with grimy adhesive tape.

What is it about the soldier? Tom thought, startled.
What is it?

The man's face squinted up. He hit the man next to him with his elbow. He muttered something.

Tom's eyes shifted to the second man. Shock drenched him. Indian beards grew slowly, and there was nothing about Apache—Joseph Celaya—to confuse him. He still looked like an Eskimo; a rather underfed one, perhaps, but any way you looked at him he was Apache!

Apache's face broke into a grin. "Hey, *amigo!*" he called. "Is that you?"

One by one they turned to look at him—Sam Worden, Terry Shanks, Leo Miles. Tom felt tears burning his eyes. Then he saw Andy start toward him, and he ran to meet him. . . .

". . . Junior said you were dead!"

"Pettis? *Junior*'s dead!"

"I saw him at an aid station at St. Vith. He said he'd walked out."

They huddled at the fire, the other Lions crowding close to listen and ask questions.

"I got shipped up to Monschau," Tom told them. "I thought it was bad there, but St.Vith was worse. —You guys look terrible," he said.

A jeep came whining down the road. Lieutenant Hammond made a cranking gesture. "Get those engines started!" An armored-force driver climbed into the boxy shell of the German assault gun. The truck drivers clambered into their cabs, and the drivers of the two quads crawled into the armored half-tracks. They were antiaircraft guns, by designation, mounting four .50-caliber machine guns firing two over two, a versatile and vicious weapon. Nava had the men raise the canvas sides of the trucks a few inches so that the steel sides could be used as shields.

The lieutenant held a handie-talkie to his ear and talked with the commander of the task force on the ridge as the jeep rolled in. Andy saw bullet holes in the hood and windshield. Two scared soldiers jumped out, one carrying a submachine gun. The lieutenant ran across the road to them.

"What's the deal?"

"We got fired on!" the man with the tommy gun said.

"What happened?"

"Couple of German scouts this side of the woods. They musta been coming down here to reconnoiter. They threw a grenade and opened fire. I emptied a clip on them. Killed them, I think."

"Didn't you make it as far as the woods?"

"Yes, sir. This happened coming back."

The lieutenant drew a trench knife, and knelt. On the smooth, frozen surface of the mud he made white scratches with the point of the knife: a *T*, then a small square strung on the upright like a bead.

"The crossbar's the ridge," he said, "where Rogers is. The vertical line is this road. The square's the farm. Show me what you saw."

The soldier touched the lower side of the square. "We went as far as the near edge of the farm. It's woods all the way there. There were no Germans in the field, but there was rifle smoke in the woods at both sides of the farm."

"How big is it?"

"Couple hundred yards each way. We parked, and reconnoitered the woods below the farm. They were clear, as far as we went. No sign of artillery, either. The ones that fired on us must have come out of the woods after we passed, going up. I guess we surprised them as much as they did us when we come tearing back."

Lieutenant Hammond rose and looked at his wristwatch. The men stood silent and scared around him. Andy had his hands clamped under his armpits for warmth. He looked at Tom.

He looks awful! he thought.

Tom gave him a weak smile. Poor kid, he was thinking.

"Rogers has brought all his trucks and most of his men to the woods at the far side of the farm," the lieutenant said. "Our mission is to open a hole through the German line and let his vehicles through."

"How much ammo have you got for the .50 calibers?" Sergeant Nava asked.

"Plenty. Once we cross the farm, we're in business. You can fell a good-sized tree with a quad, not to mention a platoon. Okay, load up," he said. "Sergeant Nava, take charge of the second truck. I'll go in the first. The assault gun will lead, then the quads. As far as I know," the lieutenant said encouragingly, "you riflemen won't have to detruck. Rogers has some paratroopers and plenty of automatic weapons. All we've got to do is open a hole for him."

The assault force lined up on the road. Tom climbed into the truck with Andy while the lieutenant made final radio contact with the task force. Then he jumped into the truck. The assault gun grated gears, rattled its track plates, and they were on the way.

Sitting close to Tom, Andy kept waiting for the old sensation of courage flowing from Tom's body to his like an electric current. Nothing happened. With something like sorrow, he knew it would never happen again. German shells had severed their private line.

Nava ordered the men in the truck to kneel on the floor and face out. The road tipped up as it approached the timber. The soldier with the tommy gun pointed.

"There's the Krauts we shot! They're dead, all right."

Andy saw the dead Germans sprawled on the snow near the road. They were garbed in white camouflage robes, now patterned with blood.

The road entered the woods, and the trucks slowed. The trees stood in clean white snow, their trunks dark and co-lumnar, like telegraph poles. No one moved, now; the men's eyes searched among the trees. The quads clattered along with a racket that Andy feared must bring down a rain of mortar shells.

"Ever seen a quad fire?" Tom asked Collins, nervously.

"Yeah. They jam," Collins said through his teeth, bitterly.

With a clinking of skid chains, the trucks halted.

Past another hundred yards of woods, Andy saw a clear-ing. The farm? From somewhere in the woods swept a gale of small-arms fire. He could see artillery bursts along the ridge. The lieutenant jumped down. With binoculars, he studied the farm and the trees beyond it. Then he told the men:

"Sit tight, now. The assault gun's going ahead to draw their fire. The quads will go next and clean out the infantry heavy weapons. The woods are too thick for them to throw any ac-curate mortar rounds."

Rattling like a bucket of stones, the assault gun lurched forward. Andy watched it leave the trees and start across the farm. It was well into the clearing when a flash lit the woods to the left. A shell screamed along the underside of the clouds, and a few yards from the assault gun the snow roared up in a black geyser. Earth and shrapnel pelted the vehicle.

Nava swore. "I thought the damned fools said they didn't have any artillery! There's an 88 in those trees!"

The assault gun stopped dead. Its turret wheeled jerkily to confront the hidden cannon. A second shell shrieked in, tearing out a chunk of pavement behind the gun and filling the air with steam and smoke. The assault gun's barrel rose slowly, raspingly.

In the truck, someone groaned, "Come on, baby—*shoot!*"

Andy saw it set itself like a shot-putter. Then the third shell came screaming from the woods. A flash swallowed the assault gun. Smoke and flame billowed; scrap metal flew into the air. When the smoke blew away, nothing was left but pieces of twisted frame and a blackened gun barrel.

The lieutenant screamed: *"Dismount! Into the ditches! Gunners, stay at your weapons!"*

The men sprawled onto the road, scrambled under the trucks and into the ditches. Andy lay in a frozen ditch, weak all over and sick at his stomach. The hidden 88 began trying to lob shells onto them. He heard them passing over and bursting a half mile away. The woods forced the cannon crew to fire high to get its shots off. Under the flying scream of the shells, the men scraped at the frozen ground with knives and bayonets. It would not be long, he knew, before the Germans knocked off the tops of a few pines and began raining tree bursts on them.

The lieutenant came crawling down the ditch. "Does anybody speak German?" he called. "I'm getting their signals. Any of you men know German?"

Andy played dead. Tom called: "Andy! They need a translator!"

Leave well enough alone, Andy was thinking. Never volunteer for anything. But already he could hear the 88 shells slamming a pathway through the tops of the pines. The detonations were closer. Soon they would be getting bursts over the road. At last he raised his head.

"Here."

The lieutenant crawled down the ditch to him, lugging a captured German radio. Voices and static rasped out of it. "Listen to this thing! Can you make out any of it?"

Voices babbled back and forth across one another incomprehensibly. Andy turned a knob and brought up a single voice. He listened intently. "It's an artillery officer. He wants an observer nearer the road." Then he heard another voice:

"Keep shelling. You're getting the range. I can see your hits from here. An observer would only be hit by fragments."

The lieutenant lay rubbing his jaw vigorously, as though to remove his beard by friction. He raised his head.

"Sergeant Nava! Any ideas?"

From under a truck, Nava replied: "All that's going to help us is a gun to knock out that 88. We'd better send somebody down to flag something on the highway. Sooner or later a tank or a fieldpiece ought to pass."

"No. The whole area's officially up for grabs. Nothing's going to pass."

"Are there any other roads to the ridge?"

"If there were, they'd have more artillery over here. Rogers thinks they must have cut a trail during the night."

The *bang-whistle-crash!* continued, round after round, on a cadence as regular as the throbbing of a frightened heart. The whistle of shrapnel was creeping closer. Andy glanced back to see how Tom was taking it. Tom lay with his head on his rifle, either resting or unconscious.

Nava's voice came again, suddenly charged with vigor: "Wait a minute! Maybe I got an idea." He crawled from under the truck to sprawl between Andy and the lieutenant.

"This boy can fake them out. He could walk right through the woods to the gun. If anybody asked where he was going, he could tell them he was looking for an aid station."

Andy felt a great throb of fear at the mere idea of walking into the German lines. "They'd believe me? In a GI uniform?"

"No, no!" Nava said. "Remember those Germans the scouts killed? We'll go down there and fit you with a camouflage suit and a German helmet and rifle."

Andy argued. What good would it do if he did reach the gun? he said desperately. It would be guarded. And even if he managed to knock out the crew, they'd man it again.

Nava gripped his arm. "Take it easy. You don't get the picture. You'll come staggering in as though you'd been wandering around wounded all day. If you get challenged, just say—how's it go?—*'Sanitäters, Sanitäters.'* You'll be loaded with grenades, see? One grenade will knock out the gun crew. Then drop another down the barrel of the gun so they can't man it again. Then take off. It's as simple as that."

From the haste with which the lieutenant was collecting grenades, it was clear that he was not asking for a volunteer. He was giving an order. Andy looked back at Tom for support. Tom was watching blearily, and listening, but Andy saw from the excitement in his face that he, too, thought it was a good idea.

"You can do it," Tom said. "It's the only way we're going to be able to get the quads in. —I'll go with him." He told the lieutenant, "If one of us doesn't get through—"

The lieutenant frowned. "One at a time," he said. "Go with him as far as the woods, but wait there for fifteen minutes."

Andy felt the quicksand pulling him down. Muscles flickered in his face. Nava was pinning grenades to his lapels like medals; then he punched Andy's chin, smiling—too hard to be playful: he was shaping him up.

"Let's go. I'll drive you down."

The camouflage suits were merely sheets draped over the dead Germans' shoulders and belted at the waist. The helmets were covered with white cloth. Nava carried the sheets and helmets into the back of the truck, where they dressed. There was a smell to the fresh blood with which Andy's camouflage robe was soaked that nauseated him. Nava's movements were quick and rough. He fastened the belt, jammed the helmet on Andy's head, then smeared some of the blood across his cheek.

"Terrific," he said approvingly. "Look the rifle over while I drive."

He drove a few hundred yards farther east along the edge of the forest, then parked. Andy climbed out and Nava pointed.

"Just follow the noise. I'll wait here. Your brother will leave in fifteen minutes if the gun's still firing."

Tom walked a few yards into the woods with him. Andy saw that he, too, was shaking. But Tom said confidently:

"You can do it, sport. Bluff them out of their socks. Anything you say will sound all right. Who makes sense in combat, anyway?"

Andy nodded. The odds were really very good. But they would have seemed even better on someone else. As he started off through the woods, Tom called after him.

"Hey! Merry Christmas!"

"Fröhliche Weinachten," Andy muttered.

He had hiked for ten minutes before he suddenly saw Germans.

Two men lay under a pine tree, gazing down the barrel of a machine gun at him. For a moment he almost sank down in shock. Surprise made him stumble. One of the gunners made a thumbs-up gesture and called encouragingly:

"Keep going. You'll see an aidman soon."

Andy blundered on. The belting roars of the gun were heavy and close, shaking barrowloads of snow from the trees. Soon he saw riflemen, and realized he was passing through a thin rearguard foxhole line. No one paid much attention to him.

Presently he saw a squad of German soldiers stringing wire. Beyond them, a team of gray-uniformed men was carrying chests of ammunition. A sudden feeling of security warmed him. He had passed the first test. He was inside the line, and to the soldiers who saw him he appeared to be a perfectly natural sight.

He changed direction, bearing squarely toward the gun. He saw a lavender warmth in the snow as it fired, felt a rush of wind past him to fill the vacuum each shot created. Then he saw a file of men bearing shells through the trees. There was another flash. Through the echoes, he heard German voices shouting. It was the gun crew calling off the numbers as they served the piece.

A moment later, through a break in the trees, he saw the long-barreled fieldpiece in a clearing.

The cannon rested on a stout truck frame with battered fenders. A lane had been cut from the clearing to the farm so that the gun barrel, deeply deflected, could shell the road that crossed it. To the left of the gun Andy saw a heap of blackened shell-cases; to the right, live shells stacked like stove-wood by a farmer's back door.

Trembling, he leaned against a tree and watched the Germans serve the 88. It resembled the celebration of a religious ceremony. Ground crewmen passed shells up to others who moved about the platform, making the same sure motions over and over: loading, closing the breech, stepping back, putting the fingers in the ears. A noncom yanked a lanyard, and a projectile flashed away in a lavender cloud of gases. The recoil bounced the men on the platform. Then they repeated the whole procedure with the next shell.

Andy drifted closer, sweat trickling down his chest. Near the mound of used shells stood an officer with field glasses. A quarter mile west, Andy saw the smoking remains of the assault gun on the road. The officer shouted a fire adjustment. A crewman spun a wheel.

"One grenade will knock out the gun crew. . . ."

Nava was wrong. It might get most of them, but with all the soldiers in these woods, the gun would soon be firing again. As for dropping a grenade down the barrel of the gun . . .

Great idea, Sarge! Andy thought helplessly. There'll be so many men around after the first grenade that I'll never get to throw a second.

Another shot roared away.

There was a distant crash and a flash in the woods. Andy thought of the quads, idling uselessly on the road. A crewman with asbestos gloves hurled the smoking shell to the ground. Another passed up a live shell from the heap at the right of the gun.

Andy looked at the shells with frustration. If I could put a bullet into the primer of one of those things— He debated moving to the right for a clear shot at the butt ends of the shells. But there was a giant flaw in the scheme: he would have to be within a few yards to be sure of hitting a target as small as the primer. If he missed, someone would kill him. And if he exploded it, the whole brass woodpile would explode in his face.

He hadn't wanted this job, anyway. He hadn't even wanted to enlist. Tom should be here, not he.

He dropped the rifle idea and reached under the sheet to clutch one of the grenades clipped to his coat. He chewed his lip, thinking sharp and hard. Could he lob one close enough?

Not from here. For if the grenade landed in even a slight depression, all the fragments would fly upward. He would have to place it by hand.

Suddenly his knees began to shake; his body knew he was going to do it even before his mind had accepted the fact.

Looking the ground over, he saw a deep slit trench only a few yards away. He drew two grenades from his coat. His anxiety subsided. It was not much, but it might be enough. Carefully, he pulled the pins and held the safety levers down. Across the clearing, he saw the tractor that had hauled the cannon across the ridge. It was too far to reach before the grenade exploded. Otherwise, except for a few small trees, he saw no shelter at all.

Well, let's go! he thought. You can't do it by leaning against a tree.

Straightening, giddy with fear, he walked past the gun and made for the ammunition. Like a man trying to warm his hands, he clamped the palmed grenades under his arms.

He faltered, as a big artilleryman rose up, staring at him. He was horse-faced, ugly. With a machine pistol, he waved Andy off. "Stay clear! This isn't the aid station."

Andy looked at him, feeling a flash of anger. I'm wounded,

and that's the best you can say? He rode the anger like a horse, strong under him but in control.

"They said it was over here, Corporal," he said plaintively.

"It isn't. It's up there—"

Andy reached the pile of shells. The artilleryman angrily started toward him. Andy sat down on the shells.

"I'm weak. I'll have to rest a minute."

The German swore at him. "I told you to take off! You're in the way. Get up."

Andy nodded. "I'm going. Merry Christmas, Corporal." He smiled in apology.

The German grunted. As Andy rose, he placed both grenades on the snow against the shells. He heard the fuses in the little iron pears begin to fry like bacon. The artilleryman walked a couple of steps closer, then scowled and turned away. Andy dug out with a yell of pure terror. He dived for the slit trench, landed flat, and buried his face in his arms.

Tom had thought nothing living could walk out of the woods after the explosion. There had been a great body-shaking pulse in the air, then a flame that boiled up to the clouds and set treetops on fire. The ground trembled. A volley of smaller explosions followed the initial blast. From the sky came a chorus of weird sighs and whistlings.

He had started through the woods. Soon he thought he heard men screaming. Then he heard the sustained, savage firing of the quads as they started across the farm. A moment later he saw the ragged soldier coming through the trees.

Tom halted in shock. The man could be German or a GI. A bloody camouflage sheet trailed from his waist. He wore no helmet, and his hair had been burned. One sleeve of his overcoat was almost completely torn from the shoulder. Tom saw that it was brown, not gray; and then, with a lift of his whole being, realized that the soldier held in his hands a pair of eyeglasses mended with tape, like Andy's. . . .

Andy looked up as Tom shouted and ran toward him. He tried to put the glasses on. Tom grappled him like a wrestler, pounding him on the back. Then he pulled Andy's arm around his neck to support him. Stumbling from side to side, they broke from the woods and onto the cleared field below.

Far to the left, Tom saw a broken column of trucks and half-tracks streaming down the road. There was no sign of the truck that had brought them down, and he thought at first that they had been left behind. Then, at the very edge of the trees, he saw the truck lunging over the ruts toward them.

Afterword

In the colossal poker game dealt personally by Adolf Hitler, the Germans from the first won most of the little pots, but consistently lost the big ones. Though several German units struggled to within a few miles of the Meuse, they were mere shock waves moving ahead of a spent projectile: the initiative had passed to the Americans.

As muddy fields and roads froze deep, American armor was at last able to maneuver at will. The skies cleared, and tons of bombs plowed the stalled Nazi columns on the roads.

Within a few more days, the great counteroffensive had run out of steam. The retreat began. Painfully, the shattered Nazi divisions groped back into Germany, leaving behind a waste of tanks, trucks, guns, and dead.

"The battle was won," writes John Toland, "not by chance, by force of numbers, or by overpowering air superiority. It was won by the GI, by his ineffable qualities. The things that made him a poor garrison soldier—independence, cockiness, love of luxury—made him finally a deadly fighter." *

* John Toland, *Battle: The Story of the Bulge* (New York: Random House, Inc., 1959).